I0554587

FROM DESTIN
WITH LOVE

Indiana Romance 4

Leanne Malloy

From Destin With Love
Leanne Malloy

Paperback Edition

Published in the United States by
Wolfpack Publishing, Las Vegas

CKN Christian Publishing
An Imprint of Wolfpack Publishing
5130 S. Fort Apache Road 215-380
Las Vegas, NV 89148

christiankindlenews.com

This book is a work of fiction. Any references to historical events, real people or real places are used fictitiously. Other names, characters, places and events are products of the author's imagination, and any resemblance to actual events, places or persons, living or dead, is entirely coincidental.

Paperback ISBN: 978-1-64734-546-4
Ebook ISBN: 978-1-64734-547-1

Library of Congress Catalog Number: 2021950483

FROM DESTIN
WITH LOVE

Dedicated to all families - those we have by birth, marriage, friendship, work ties, social groups, and so many other possibilities. They are God's comfort as we live this amazing life.

Prologue

"It's my twin, Courtney B!" the little girl shrieked, running through the fluffy snow to meet Courtney Bledsoe. Little Courtney Stanfield had bonded with Courtney when they met at her friend Lauren's for Thanksgiving dinner. Lauren had continued her parents' tradition of sharing her table with those who didn't have family to visit over the holiday weekend. Since the Stanfields usually went home to California at Christmas, they had joined Courtney and the other adult "orphans" at Lauren's that year. Once young Courtney learned they shared a name, she'd forever idolized Courtney B, as she called her. "Hi, honey," Courtney said, hugging her energetic friend. "Are you enjoying the snow?"

"You bet. Watch me make snow angels, Courtney B." As the girl relished being in the chilly snow, Courtney smiled at the heavily pregnant woman in front of her.

"How are you doing, Elaine? When's that baby due?"

"He's overdue, as of yesterday," Elaine Stanfield

said, massaging her massive belly. "I thought a walk in the freezing Indiana cold would help things along. If nothing else, it will tire Courtney out."

"I can understand why that would be a good thing," Courtney said with a grin. "Good luck, Elaine. If you need any help with babysitting, let me know. My 'twin' and I can keep each other company while you tend to the little man." Courtney waved and headed toward her car.

Rubbing her hands together was an exercise in futility, Courtney told herself. Walking her usual daily laps around the historic Gordon, Indiana, city park in a minus five-degree wind chill while expecting to stay warm was not only futile, but foolish. Courtney's Raynaud's disease was causing her digits to redden, whiten, and numb by the second. So why was she punishing herself like this? Unlike her buddy Courtney Stanfield, she had no tolerance for winter weather.

Drew's email yesterday had been her undoing. He had scolded her for the lack of referrals to his psychiatry practice, despite her insistence that she was sending every Gordon Community College student in need of his services. She was not about to compromise herself with bogus, unwarranted referrals. Drew's message, arriving at the end of the day Friday, ensured her weekend would not be the relaxing escape she had hoped for.

Missing her mom more than ever, Courtney quickened her pace and hunkered down against the Indiana winter wind. Her parents' deaths over four years ago in a car accident had been the ultimate tragedy in her otherwise carefree life. Her mother would have known just the right thing to say to

Drew. In her heart, she knew her mom would have told him to straighten up and to act like the ethical professional he professed to be. Too bad Courtney couldn't say those words on her own.

Her woolen mittens and socks, in addition to hand and foot warmers, weren't doing the job on her cold extremities. She had to get back to her car soon, or she would pay the price of fiery fingers and toes once she was home. What she wouldn't give to live in a warm climate. Florida, Arizona, or even South Carolina would guarantee Courtney's comfort during the winter months. Unfortunately, moving was not in the cards for her. She and Drew were a couple, and she hoped for a proposal soon. After all, he was the one constantly referring to their future together, right?

Comfortably in her car with the heater cranked up, Courtney answered a call from her friend Annie Upton. "You're up early, Annie," she teased. "It's Saturday. My recollection is you sleep until noon on the weekends."

Annie laughed, though without her usual joyful timbre. "Yeah, I'm up, Court. Is this a good time to talk?"

"It's fine. I'm in my car after my walk around the park."

"As if winter in Indiana isn't uncomfortable enough," Annie chided. "You couldn't walk at the fitness center? Or the indoor track on campus? Your fingers and toes must be hurting."

"They are," Courtney admitted. "But they'll thaw out soon. I've got the ingredients for cinnamon rolls laid out on my counter at home. Working that dough will warm me up fast. What's on your mind?"

A long pause served as the initial answer to Courtney's question. Annie finally spoke. "I've been all over the board about whether to tell you this. Ben said I should, and I agree. Yesterday, when I was doing supervision with the new nurse practitioner, she got a call from Drew."

"That shouldn't be a big deal," Courtney said. "Leslie refers students to Drew, just like I do."

"True. But this call wasn't like that, Court. They talked for almost a half hour, while I sat and tended to emails on my phone. And they were chummy, you know? Leslie actually giggled a few times. It was off, Courtney. It wasn't a professional discussion at all. I think she let the call drag on because I'd just told her we needed to review more of her charts than

usual. I was noticing referrals to Drew for kids that had a bad day, not true depression. I was ready to rip into her, and she knew it."

Annie stopped talking again, though she was obviously not finished. "Okay, buddy. Here's the rest. When she hung up, she checked her cell phone and fake-whispered, 'He's such a sweetheart.' She looked up at me and pretended I wasn't supposed to hear that. She meant to do it, Court. I got the message loud and clear. Drew's a pig."

"I see." Courtney rested her cold forehead on the steering wheel. "Thanks for calling, Annie. I realize it was hard for you to tell me all this. But it's good that I know. I've been getting mixed signals from Drew for a while now. Hopefully it's just a harmless flirtation to help him get more patients from the college."

"Maybe. Or maybe it's more than that. Keep your eyes open, Courtney. My Italian instincts are usually on target."

The friends ended the chat, and Courtney knew Annie was right. Drew was on the prowl, and not just for new clients. What was she going to do?

Her phone jingled again, this time with Drew's name displayed on the caller ID. His timing had always been excellent. "Hi there, Drew," she said with deliberate perkiness. "Happy Saturday. Do we have plans for tonight?"

Another pause ensued. This pattern of her callers hesitating to speak wasn't good. Finally, Drew answered.

"We've got to talk, Courtney," he said. "I just don't see us together for the long haul anymore. I'm not ready to commit to anyone at this point. You're a great woman. It's me, not you."

If only he'd used a few more cliches, she'd have enough to embroider them on a designer pillow. Drew had never been an original thinker. But first, she had to answer him.

"I'm not surprised," she said with a calm tone she didn't feel. "You've been distant and even mean lately, Drew. So, it's for the best. Take good care."

Courtney ended the call before Drew could reply with any more trite, self-aggrandizing excuses. He continued to call, so she turned her phone off. Drew Clifton could speak into the void of her voicemail forever as far as she was concerned.

Now it wasn't just her hands and feet that were cold with needle-sharp pains. Her heart was a tight block in her chest. And the tears were freezing on her cheeks as they came down.

Chapter One

Six months later

Courtney walked toward the Destin Diabetes Care Clinic with equal amounts of resolve and trepidation. Her kitten heels tapped lightly on the designer cobblestone walk while the skirt of her cotton dress swayed in the gentle April breeze. Topping her floral outfit was a pastel blue cardigan, an outfit appropriate for her role as the new psychologist at the clinic. Similar to her clothing choices at her past post at Gordon Community College, her attire was professional, but not off-putting to vulnerable patients. Her coppery red hair was done in a fashionable messy bun. Now if the clinic director would agree she could be a useful addition, life would be good. Her dream was about to come true. A great job, a beachside condo, and an escape from the cold weather and a certain colder man in her hometown of Gordon, Indiana, would combine to make for a perfect life. As if there were such a thing.

Thanks to information she'd gotten from the office manager, Dr. Greg McClure had deferred to his father, the founder of the clinic, about Courtney's employment. Just before his retirement, Dr. Eric McClure had been to a conference that discussed the value of a comprehensive in-house team approach to the care of patients with diabetes. Greg had argued against the inclusion of a psychologist to their staff, but Courtney was hired by Eric while Greg was on vacation. Greg's first day back on the job happened to coincide with Courtney's first day at the clinic. Based on the email she'd received detailing her packed schedule of appointments, she should be busy enough to avoid Greg entirely, which she prayed was a good omen.

Courtney paused outside the clinic, studying the exterior for clues about the reception she would receive. Flower boxes decorated the front windows, an unusual touch for a medical building. The stucco and frame two-story building looked almost residential, the creamy color accented by aqua trim. Courtney took a deep breath and entered through the wooden door, again a contrast to the medical entries of Indiana, which were usually glass and metal. She surveyed the waiting room, noting a continuation of the outdoor colors – turquoise chairs and sofas, and ivory accent tables topped with contemporary magazines. There was no evidence of the usual proprietary medical literature, which often featured articles about the newest drugs and weight-loss plans. Courtney thought the signs for a warm welcome looked good so far.

"Hi there, Dr. Bledsoe," a pleasant silver-haired woman said. "We met the day you interviewed, but you may not remember. I'm Jackie Kindrick, the receptionist, scheduler, factotum, and general know-it-all around here. Welcome to our team."

"I do remember you," Courtney said. "You were very generous when I was interviewing. I had no idea there would be so many staff members with input on my hire. The day went smoothly, in large part to your shepherding me around and soothing my nerves. Thanks so much for all you did."

"You're very welcome. You were my favorite candidate, Dr. Bledsoe. The others were so impressed with themselves. I just couldn't see them dealing with our challenging patients day in and day out. Have you found a place to live yet?"

Courtney smiled at Jackie, grateful again for her kindness. "Yes, it's my dream home. I've got a condo on Miramar Beach. I drink my coffee each morning on the balcony while I enjoy the gentle sun and ocean waves. It's quite a change from Indiana."

As she was talking, the front door flew open. Dr. Greg McClure's rushed entry served to announce his presence. Courtney recognized him from the photo on the clinic's website, but he was better looking than she'd thought. The picture hadn't captured his startling green eyes, nor his muscular build. He looked like a serious bodybuilder; a type Courtney had dealt with plenty of times. Usually, they were so into their physiques, special diets, and workout schedules they had no time for relationships. Greg McClure was a looker all right, but at present he seemed annoyed.

"Dr. Bledsoe, I presume. You bought a condo on Miramar Beach? Do you realize what you're in for? The minute they find out you're a local, the snowbirds will pester you for the entire winter season. Then for the month of March, you'll deal with all the kids partying on spring break. And storm season won't be a picnic so close to the water. Typical northerner mistake." Greg ended his tirade with an exaggerated head shake.

"Yes, I'm Dr. Bledsoe," Courtney said calmly. *So much for avoiding this guy due to my busy schedule.* "Yes, I bought a condo on the beach. Yes, I like older people, so the snowbirds won't be a problem. Yes, I'm aware of spring break antics, having just left the college environment, so I plan to rent my unit out during that time, with the caveat that renters must be over twenty-five. I can couch surf with friends and make some extra money. Hurricane season will certainly beat the winter sub-zero temperatures and ice storms in Indiana. So, it's going to be fine. But thanks for your friendly concern."

Jackie laughed and then turned away at Greg's glare. "Let me show you the break room and your office, Dr. Bledsoe. Dr. McClure has to settle in before his first patient. He's been away on vacation with his lady friend."

"Watch it, Jackie," Dr. McClure growled. "My dad let you get away with that sort of familiarity, but I won't."

"Sorry, Dr. McClure," Jackie said, her eyes twinkling and clearly not sorry at all. "I've put your coffee on your desk, so you're ready for the day. We're booked solid."

Courtney and Jackie toured the back office area, and had the boxes Courtney had brought in from her car emptied within a half hour. Courtney decided to take a risk. Jackie seemed like a safe person to confide in.

"So, the culture here is to use 'Doctor' titles at all times? No first names?"

Jackie shrugged and looked a little wistful. "Dr. Eric, which is what we all called him, was less formal than his son. Under his watch you would have been Dr. Courtney. But Dr. Greg is more formal, as you've just witnessed. It's probably a good idea to be precise with his title unless he tells you differently."

Courtney paused, hoping Jackie would continue. The factotum took the hint. "When Dr. Eric started the clinic, each day had a rhythm. We saw our patients, they took their scripts for meds, repeat labs, and other services, and they rescheduled. The length of time until their next appointment was dependent on how they were doing."

"That sounds about right," Courtney said. "How are things different now?"

"Since Dr. Eric went to the conference, he's added staff, including you. We now have a dietitian who comes in four days a week, and she'll soon be full-time. Our nurses are happy about that, since the patients didn't generally follow through with the referrals to the Destin hospital dietitians. We'll be adjusting to you next, but I think that will be easy," Jackie concluded, winking.

Courtney wondered what Jackie wasn't saying and went with her gut. "You're saying the nurses are happy with the changes, and you seem to be as well. What about Dr. Greg McClure?"

"He's had a bit of a tough time," Jackie admitted. "He contradicts the dietitian sometimes, but she's a Certified Diabetes Care and Education Specialist, like you. Her knowledge of current dietary recommendations is second to none."

Thank you, Lord, for prompting me to get my CDCES credential, Courtney thought. In fact, Annie had seemed to be the one doing the prompting when she was applying for promotion at Gordon Community College and needed to document continuing education. Annie wanted company during the classes and convinced Courtney that learning about healthy habits and nutrition would help in her work with many college students, not just those with diabetes. Since Drew had been "busy" so often, and since she loved learning new things, Courtney had done the training. Getting the hours of experience had been a challenge, but she'd volunteered at a comprehensive health center on the eastside of Indianapolis for several months during her vacation time from the college. Passing the qualifying exam had also been tough, but both she and Annie were now CDCESs.

"What happens when Dr. McClure disagrees with a staff recommendation?" she asked.

Looking away, Jackie seemed to be searching for the right thing to say to a new hire on her first day. "It depends. Sometimes he lets it go and things are fine. A few times, he's reminded the dietitian, Jessica, that her place is to follow his lead, not make her own diet plan for patients."

"Kind of contradicts the whole point of having a dietitian, doesn't it?" Courtney was concerned and not afraid of letting Jackie know. Greg's style with the dietitian would probably be his style with her. Maybe she should have rented an apartment instead of buying a condo so soon. This job could be short-lived.

"It's not a big deal," Jackie hedged. "Dr. McClure doesn't like change, and we're all still adjusting. It will be fine."

"Got it," Courtney said. Since Jackie looked increasingly tense, she changed the subject. "What would you like me to call you? Mrs. Kindrick? Miss Jackie?"

"Oh, my," Jackie said, her face full of wonder. "No one has ever bothered to ask me. You don't know how much it means. An office full of medical types has a distinct pecking order, and I'm on the bottom. Anyway, you can call me Jackie. I'm fine with that."

"Jackie it is, then." Studying the paper on her desk, Courtney continued. "My schedule printout says I have an hour until my first patient. I think I'll play with your electronic charting program to get up to speed."

"It's pretty intuitive," Jackie said. "Though I hate it when tech salespeople say that.

It's usually a red flag that there's nothing intuitive about their product at all." The women laughed, and Jackie went back to her desk.

Feeling comfortable with the electronic medical record system after a few minutes, Courtney surveyed her office. Small, but nicer than some she'd been assigned in the past. Her desk sat to the side, allowing room for a tiny loveseat and two stuffed armchairs. A coffee table fronted the seating choices. Nondescript art graced each wall. The paint color was a formerly trendy taupe, with baseboards accented in a lighter shade. Most notably, her furniture pieces had some significant age on them, in contrast to the newness of the waiting room.

My office is the hand-me-down spot. I wonder

what would happen if I hung my own pictures or painted everything a light shade of blue grey? I could use Annie's expertise; she'd have this place looking wonderful. The thought of her good friend from GCC brought a wave of homesickness to Courtney. Had she made a big mistake coming to Destin?

Her door opened, and Dr. McClure entered with a patient chart. Ignoring pleasantries, which Courtney noted was his pattern, he began, "I'm sending Alice Haig in, since you're free for another twenty minutes. She shouldn't take long. Just give her a lecture about the need for her to lose weight. She's sixty-five, obese, and her blood sugars are elevated. A little self-control is all she needs."

Courtney knew better, and she wondered why Dr. McClure didn't. "Weight loss is not a simple science, as we all know, Doctor. Willpower is also a complex thing. I'll talk to her, and we'll have a baseline for our future work together. My sense is you've already given her plenty of lectures about the need to reduce her weight. Correct?"

Offering no response, Dr. McClure turned on his heel. As she watched him leave, Courtney shuddered. He was going to be a tough sell for psychological services. Hopefully she wouldn't be fired within her first two weeks.

I knew she'd be difficult. Why Dad wanted a psychologist is beyond me. All these psych types do is coddle the patients who just need a good butt-kicking.

He had to admit, though, that lecturing Alice Haig had been ineffective. She agreed with all of his points then proceeded to gain another pound or two by her next appointment. In fact, many of his other patients weren't doing that well either. One in particular, a sixteen-year-old girl on an insulin pump, made him anxious. Maybe Dr. Courtney Bledsoe could help her. But he had his doubts.

The psychologist his father had been so impressed with was a puzzle to him. She was pretty, almost striking with that red hair, but what had Dad seen in her? She was a CDCES, sure, but she hadn't worked extensively with diabetic patients. She'd worked with college kids, and he doubted their issues were that challenging. Probably homesickness, boyfriend troubles, and changing majors. Trivial issues compared to a life-threatening illness. And she didn't want his input, that was clear. He'd have to remind her of the line of authority around here. He had the final say about patients, and it was *his* medical degree and license on the line. Plus, what was the deal with the dress and sweater? They looked good on her, highlighting what appeared to be a great body, but he believed a tailored suit was more appropriate for the clinic setting. He wondered if she were a Millennial. He'd heard they did their own thing, even in professional roles. No, he'd seen her new-hire paperwork. She was thirty-five, his age and not technically a Millennial. Still single, also unusual.

Shaking his head, he realized he was getting distracted by her appearance. It was time to buckle down. He'd have Jackie arrange a meeting with Courtney, so he could fill her in on his expectations. He had to make the clinic a success now that Dad was retired. He could handle the pressure, but he wasn't about to let a new psychologist undermine his efforts.

Since he'd spent little time with Alice, he reviewed the charts of the remaining patients for the day. Mandy Eller, the sixteen-year-old he'd been worried about, was next on his schedule. At that moment, Jackie turned on his call light, indicating Mandy and her mother were in the exam room.

"Hi, Dr. McClure," Cathy Eller said. "It's so good to see you at last. I've been really upset about Mandy's glucose readings."

Surveying the vital signs, current weight, and the lab values in Mandy's chart, Greg looked at the girl. "Are *you* worried, Mandy? How are you feeling?"

"Great, as always," Mandy replied, pasting a smile on her face while rolling her eyes. "My sugars are a little whacky, but that's because I'm growing, right? No big deal."

Greg looked at Mandy. He was sure she was faking her sunny demeanor. Her blonde hair was curled in what he assumed was the latest style, falling in waves around her shoulders. She was dressed in fashionable torn jeans with a midriff top exposing tight abs and a belly ring. She was obviously fit and toned, which he respected. Mandy's appearance radiated good health. But as a veteran kid with diabetes, diagnosed at age six, she knew her glucose values were cause for concern. She was hiding something, and he knew what it was. Proving it was tougher.

"No, Mandy, you know the sugars aren't okay. Lots of things can influence them, including a growth spurt. My sense is there's more going on. Maybe another stint at diabetes camp would help you sort things out."

"Absolutely not!" Mandy shouted. "I won't go back to camp this summer. I'd be the oldest kid there. I refuse to be an unpaid counselor while the elementary kids learn how to use their insulin pumps. Anyway, I've got a full-time job starting in May. There's no need, or time, for diabetes camp."

Knowing Mandy's oppositional pattern, Greg stayed calm. "A job? That's great, Mandy. What will you be doing?"

"I'm a hostess at the new steakhouse on Highway 98 in Santa Rosa Beach," Mandy announced. "I've been subbing a little while I train. It's so much fun. I meet all sorts of people, and staff gets free food. You wouldn't believe all the different ways there are to cook a steak."

His suspicions confirmed, Greg continued to play along. "I'm glad to hear you like it, Mandy. All that gourmet food around would tempt me too much. How do you manage it?"

"I have an iron will; just ask my Mom," Mandy retorted, looking unsettled. "Right, Mom?"

"Yes, a very strong will," Cathy responded. "But I agree with Dr. McClure. All the foods, aromas, and appetizing presentations would be too much for me. That's why I'm worried."

Cathy looked tired, almost spent. Her jeans were baggy, and her eyes filled with tears as she talked. Mandy was scaring her. As a single mom, widowed last year, Greg knew Cathy had to shoulder the burden of Mandy's illness alone.

Cathy had obviously figured out Mandy's tactics as well. Mandy was playing with the settings on her insulin pump after she ate too much, restricting her needed dose in order to maintain her weight. Teens with diabetes usually experimented with this strategy until they learned about the dangers involved.

In the short term, their sugars ran too high, often landing them in a diabetic coma. If they survived those crises, continued insulin shortages would lead to an increased risk of long-term complications like blindness, neuropathies, and even amputation of limbs. If they were especially unlucky, they could die while comatose.

But Greg knew telling all that to a pretty sixteen-year-old with an exciting life ahead of her was futile. As futile as sending her back to diabetes camp. She'd heard it all before. He and her mom needed help with Mandy.

"Excuse me, ladies," he said. "I'm going to consult with Dr. Bledsoe. Be right back."

As Greg turned down the hallway to Courtney's office, he saw her walking Alice back to the appointment desk. Each woman laughed softly, and as Alice exited the waiting area, she gave Courtney a hug.

Great, he thought. *They're best buddies, but Alice won't make any changes.*

"Dr. Bledsoe, I need a moment. I've got Mandy Eller and her mother in my office. I'm sure Mandy's been skipping insulin to avoid weight gain. She may even be bingeing, since she's got a new job at a restaurant. I'd like to add them to your caseload. Tomorrow, if possible."

His polite request seemed to have confused her. After a pause, Courtney answered, "Of course, Dr. McClure. My next appointment was cancelled due to family illness. I can see them now if you want. If your theory is correct, I'll enter 'Other Specified Feeding or Eating Disorder' as my diagnosis. I just hate the term *diabulimia,* and it's not recognized by insurers anyway. You okay with that?"

Marveling at her willingness to see Mandy immediately, and at her knowledge of the girl's condition, Greg smiled. "I'm more than okay, I appreciate your help. I'll admit Mandy is one of those patients who keeps me up at night. She's impulsive, charming, and thinks she knows her way around her illness. That sort of false expertise is common with kids who've dealt with diabetes during their formative years. Now teenage rebellion adds to the mix, in addition to the desire to be like everyone else. Her mother, Cathy, who is a recent widow, is at the end of her tether. You're taking on a lot with them."

Courtney smiled, looking at him directly with her crystal-blue eyes, shocking him with her quiet beauty. "It's my job," she said. "No magic cures, but with time and hard work, maybe Mandy can figure out how to be healthy and still have some fun."

Greg paused, then backtracked from his request. "On second thought, let's schedule Mandy and her mom for tomorrow. They're finishing an intense appointment with me, and then they see the dietitian. I'm going to assign them homework to review Mandy's current treatment regimen. That way they'll be ready for you, and you'll have time to get up to speed on Mandy's history. What do you think?"

"I think it's a good plan," Courtney said. "Mandy will need time to regroup. Her mother probably has other things to do today. I'll see them first thing in the morning."

What a first day, Courtney reflected as she sat on her balcony watching the frothy waves kiss the white sand. *My caseload was about what I expected, except for Mandy. She's the highest risk of any person with diabetes – fiddling with her insulin dosage so she can eat at will. Of course, it doesn't work that way.*

After finishing the leftover shrimp scampi from last night's feast at the beachside restaurant only steps away, Courtney was tempted to bake. Her go-to stress reliever was usually helpful after a tough day. She had a new recipe for New York cheesecake, and all the ingredients were in her fridge or pantry. But she knew she needed a walk instead. Sandy beach walks were better than those in chilly Indiana, and a walk always helped her think. After her walk she would call her sister in Gordon. Sherry was her sister, best friend, and therapist all rolled into one kind, loving woman. Without Sherry, Courtney often wondered how she'd ever have been able to get over Drew Clifton. She remembered the arctic day that began with Annie's warning and concluded with Drew's cowardly phone call. Courtney had been so sure, so convinced they could work out their differences. Wrong.

Because it wasn't "differences" that ended the relationship. It was a fundamental divergence in core values. Courtney believed in God, family, and work. Drew honored those beliefs, apart from putting God before family, work, and ultimately money. Drew had started a psychiatric clinic in Gordon, at first meshing well with Courtney's counseling department at Gordon Community College. For a year, referrals between them had been smooth, benefitting the students at GCC. Their nonprofessional relationship had also flourished, with Drew mentioning that marriage would happen as soon as he felt stable financially. But then Drew began to slowly poach her therapy clients, saying his practice would serve them better than her tiny clinic at the college. It took her a while, too long, to realize the students Drew kept on his roster were those with generous health insurance benefits. Their arguments had increased, eventually causing Drew to question her love for him. Courtney also questioned his love for her, as he began to seek referrals from the new campus NP. Leslie became his new partner in mental health, and in the bedroom.

His father, power-hungry Dan Clifton, had egged him on, always focusing on Drew's need for income to pay his student loan debts and grow his practice. Dan viewed Courtney's ethical objections to Drew's practices as evidence of her disloyalty. And once his dad used the word "disloyal", Courtney was effectively out of Drew's life. After a quick job hunt, Courtney found the job in Destin. It was time to leave Gordon and all the memories it held.

I'm a crack psychologist, she thought as she blew out a defeated sigh. *I was sure Drew would realize his clinic could coexist with the GCC counseling center, and that our love would weather his dad's interference. Didn't happen.*

As she reached the mile mark and made her turn, her pager jingled its perky melody. She looked at the number, not recognizing it. Knowing it wouldn't be wise to ignore a first-day page, she entered the number on her cell phone, hoping the message was meant for someone else.

"Courtney, are you there?" Greg asked. "I'm on my way to the emergency department at Twin Cities Hospital in Niceville. Cathy Eller called. Mandy was admitted in severe ketoacidosis, but they think she'll be okay. Evidently, she filled a shift at work and ate the entire afternoon and evening with no insulin, of course. Could you meet me at the emergency department? I think it's important Mandy and Cathy meet you in person now, since they won't be at the appointment tomorrow."

Shocked at Greg's distress, Courtney replied, "Of course. I'll be there as soon as I can. I'm Google-mapping the distance on my phone as we speak. I should arrive in about a half hour."

"Thanks, Courtney. I never should have let Mandy leave the office without seeing you today. She needed stabilizing. I just didn't get it."

Aware that Greg had called her Courtney twice, she answered, "No sense in second-guessing all that. Teens are tough to pin down, even teens not battling diabetes. Their mood swings can be vicious. I'll see you soon."

"Sorry to page you on your first day, but I think the Ellers need to have us in the ED with them. It will show Cathy we're committed to Mandy's care and that she's not alone. And hopefully, it will bring home to Mandy what a mess she's making of her health."

"I agree," Courtney said. "Good call. I'm on my way." Power-walking back to her condo, she debated changing clothes. No, her skinny jeans and printed tropical shirt were fine. The key was to get to Mandy quickly, not project a certain image.

And what about Greg? He's showing a side I didn't see today at the office. Maybe he cares more about his patients than I realized.

Chapter Two

Greg watched as the new clinic psychologist made her way across the hospital parking lot. In contrast to her quiet confidence at work earlier today, Courtney seemed hesitant, almost traumatized. Her eyes were watering. What could that be about? Was she worried about her ability to provide care for Mandy and her mother? Had his father made a big mistake when he hired Dr. Bledsoe? He pushed his doubts aside for the moment. At this point, his focus had to be on Mandy.

"Did you have any trouble finding the hospital?" he asked, using small talk to allow Courtney to compose herself. "Sometimes the roads are confusing to northerners, what with our bridges and turnoffs."

"No, the directions were spot on," Courtney answered. "What's the latest with Mandy's condition?"

"The news is good for now," Greg said. "They'll keep her overnight, but she's stable. She's full of remorse, mostly due to her mom's agony, which is palpable. I wish I could be sure it would last, but Mandy's been a handful since I've known her."

"Are we going to be able to see her? Or should we let Mandy and Cathy have some private time?"

"We'll see them. Cathy really wants to meet you. I have hospital privileges, but since you aren't credentialed yet, stick to introductions and pleasantries for now. It's important for Mandy to associate your name with a face. And Cathy needs someone in her corner. I think you'll be great with them, provided we can keep Mandy stable for more than a few weeks."

"Will do," Courtney said as they walked into the hospital. Greg noticed her deep breath and the sudden square set of her shoulders. Something had spooked her, but he didn't think it was Mandy. For some unknown reason, hospitals had her on the defensive.

Entering Mandy's room, Greg assessed the sad twosome in the center. Mandy was in bed, hooked to intravenous fluids, weeping softly. Cathy stroked Mandy's hair as she spoke softly to her daughter.

"It's going to be okay," Cathy said. "You made a mistake, but that's how we learn. I love you so much, sweetie. I know you're in pain, the kind a mom can't help, but we'll find what you need, honey. Just keep trying."

"I'm a moron, Mom," Mandy said with a sniffle. "The food smelled so good, but I can't get fat. You know how that will add to my diabetes mess. So, shorting the insulin was a good idea, at least in my mind. You say I'll learn, but I'm not so sure. I do know one thing, though. I can't get fat. I'm already a freak who's hooked up to a machine 24/7. Everyone will really make fun if I gain weight. You can't believe what the fat girls go through. It's way worse than having diabetes."

Greg decided it was time to interrupt or they'd have a full-blown therapy session going strong. "Hey, Mandy, what gives? Wasn't it enough to see my charming face in the office today? Now I'm getting paged about you and have to drive all the way to Niceville." His eyes betrayed his concern, and Mandy smiled.

"I'm sorry, Dr. McClure," she said. "You were right about what I was doing with my insulin pump. I just got caught this time."

"We'll deal with that when you're stronger," Greg said. "I did want you to meet Dr. Bledsoe, though, so you'd be familiar with her when you work together at the clinic. She's new to our practice."

Courtney smiled and extended her hand to Mandy. "It's good to meet you," she said. "And your mom as well." Directing her focus to Cathy, she asked, "It's been a long day, huh?"

"One of the longest," Cathy replied. "But my baby is going to be fine, which is all that matters."

Stifling a yawn, Mandy broke in, "My mom is the best. She's sad about my dad, and now I put her through this. I'm worthless."

"You're exhausted, and your mom's not far behind you," Courtney said softly. "Why don't we let you both rest. We'll meet soon at the clinic."

Greg was grateful Courtney had ended Mandy's dramatic self-loathing. There would be time for uncovering all those feelings during a structured psychotherapy session. He also wondered about Mandy's mental status. She couldn't be tracking too well given her physical state. After the usual small talk, he and Courtney left the room.

"Are you okay, Courtney?" he asked as they walked to her car. "You were a little tense at first."

"Good observation," Courtney replied. "I hate hospitals. Lots of sad memories from my parents' car accident. It's been nearly five years since they died, but sometimes the memories flood back. This place looks a lot like the hospital in Gordon. They must have used the same cookie-cutter architect."

Courtney shrugged, then continued. "But I'm fine. Once I saw Mandy and Cathy, the professional in me took over. They seem to have a good bond, though they may be a little enmeshed. It happens a lot with chronically ill kids and their parents."

Stunned, Greg stopped mid-stride. "I'm so sorry, Courtney. I had no idea about your parents. The good thing is we rarely visit patients when they're hospitalized. Your work will be solely at the office."

Despite his assurances, Greg wondered what else was going on. He knew grief could linger, but after five years, Courtney's response to the hospital seemed extreme. He was sure she was grieving something else, something or someone more recent.

Courtney's blue eyes turned dark, almost black. "I'm competent to do hospital visits whenever needed. As you said earlier, I just need to get credentialed. No biggie. I've had privileges at several hospitals in Indiana."

"Again, I'm sorry. I didn't mean to offend." He looked at Courtney and took a risk. "It's been a convoluted evening. I'm wound tight. Any chance you'd like to go out for a quick drink? I guarantee there will be no office talk, just a chance to relax a little."

Courtney's eyes lightened as she considered his request. "Sure, that would be nice. You can introduce me to Destin's best bar food. I had just finished supper when you paged. Did you get to eat?"

"As a matter of fact, I didn't. Let's go to Crabby's. Terrible name, but good, greasy comfort food and beautiful ocean views. Maybe you can get a salad or whatever."

"Whatever," Courtney said with an eye roll.

Directions were shared, and Courtney followed Greg to the restaurant. They were seated in time to watch the sun descend into the horizon, followed by the brief, mystical green fire. Courtney was enchanted.

"Does the beauty of that ever get old? The colors are both soothing and stimulating. And with the waves breaking, the experience is almost hypnotic. I love it here."

"No, it never gets old," Greg said, referring both to the sun and to the beauty in front of him. He'd been aware of her allure in the office, but now was different. She was clad in those tight jean-legging things, with a snug shirt completing what must be her usual after-work attire. She wore them well, very well.

"Are you still with me?" Courtney asked. "You left for a minute."

"Still here," Greg said. "So, are you alone in the world? Any brothers or sisters to help as you miss your mom and dad?"

"One sister, Sherry," Courtney said. "A wonderful woman. She's thirty, lives in Gordon, and is engaged. I'll be needing some time off for her wedding in the fall, by the way."

Sipping the amber liquid with a barely noticeable shudder, Courtney sat back and gave Greg what felt like the stink-eye. "And what about you, Dr. Mc-Clure? Any family around other than your dad?"

"My mother died when I was in college," he answered. "She had a type of cancer they've since developed successful treatments for. My dad soldiers on, up to now mostly at the clinic. With his retirement I'm not sure how he'll fill the days. I'm worried about him, and a little angry at the same time."

"Angry? Why are you angry? Because he hired me?"

Breathing hard, Courtney looked both anxious and indignant at the same time. Greg liked what he saw. This woman wasn't a cool psychologist at all. She had a temper.

"Not exactly," he said. "The clinic has been adjusting to the ever-changing insurance payment systems. Sometimes our cash flow isn't what it should be, but our accountant says things will even out. It's just that another professional salary wasn't what we needed at this point. Dad thought differently. He was convinced about the value of a psychologist on staff."

Courtney continued to stare. "Well, I'm truly sorry about your mother, Dr. McClure. Cancer is such a tragedy. I'm glad your dad is still here for you. And I'm really glad he hired me! Trust me, having a psychologist on your team will be worth it. Patients respond well to the chance to receive care at one location. The medical system can be stifling."

"Speaking of getting care, what did you think of the Ellers?"

"As I said, they love each other deeply but are likely drowning in that overwhelming love, tempered with their grief. As Mandy wants more independence, Cathy is going to have to trust her.

Given what I've heard about Mandy, that will be a challenge."

Courtney took another sip of her bourbon. Greg had been shocked when she'd ordered it. How many women liked bourbon? Usually his dates ordered white wine like it was their job. Courtney was different, in a lot of ways.

"I have another thought, Dr. McClure. Since we're talking shop, despite your assurance we wouldn't, let's think about Mandy's care. Did you hear what she said about getting fat? I think we should refer her to an eating disorders program. Would Cathy agree to that?"

Greg reddened. "Refer her out? Are you kidding? I just told you our cash flow was iffy, and your response is to get rid of a patient?"

What was with this guy? He'd acted as though Mandy was his top priority in the world but wouldn't consider the treatment she so obviously needed. Cash flow concerns paled in comparison to his gigantic ego. He'd paged her on her first day, directed her hospital interventions with Mandy, and then placated her with the offer of a drink. Despite her initial hope of him being human when they talked in the hospital parking lot, Greg McClure was living up to her first impression – unfairly handsome and hugely self-absorbed. To top off his arrogance, he'd called her Courtney several times but seemed happy to let her address him as Dr. McClure.

And she hoped her reaction to the hospital hadn't given her away. She'd always grieve her parents, but her tearfulness was because the building looked exactly like the clinic Drew had built in Gordon. Despite her belief in him, he was cheap to the core, always thinking about making money, even to the point of using stock architectural plans along with the most inexpensive materials. In fact, Greg Mc-Clure was sounding more like Drew by the second.

Gathering herself, she set her drink on the table. "You wouldn't be getting rid of a patient," she said. "You would still provide her primary medical care. The eating disorders clinic, though, could supplement that in ways we can't do at our office."

Greg took a bite of his chili fries. Sauce and beans dripped on his dress shirt, and Courtney felt vindicated at karma taking a hand. Maybe the universe was telling him to learn what an interdisciplinary team actually meant.

"I see," he said slowly, using his thin paper napkin to mop the stain into an even bigger mess. "So, I'd provide Mandy's diabetes care, but the psych stuff would be done elsewhere. Doesn't sound at all like coordinated care to me."

"It's *appropriate* care," Courtney countered. "We each have our own skill sets. You're a pro in the diabetes world, but not in the eating disorders realm. I'm a good generalist psychologist and CDCES, but a patient as risky as Mandy needs care from an ED team, not one person. She probably also needs group therapy, which we can't provide."

Courtney paused, then continued her argument. "Mandy is just the type of patient I referred to the ED center in Indianapolis when I was working at GCC. A kid like Mandy would fail miserably in a college setting. Think about it. In barely a year, Mandy will be ready for college. If she continues to binge with food and purge with insulin, she'll never make it." Thinking about all her referrals to Drew, she gulped and shook her head. When would she ever be over his betrayal?

Courtney picked up her drink, took a healthy swallow, and planted the glass on the table. Greg leaned in, covered her hand with his, and looked at her with what might have been tenderness. She'd given herself away; Greg knew she was suffering about more than her parents' deaths. The feel of his hand over hers was a surprise, a very pleasant one.

"Relax, Courtney," he said. "I understand what you're saying. Thanks for helping me grasp what Mandy needs." He left his hand on hers until she jerked it away. Knowing he was again exerting control, Courtney decided to take it back.

"You're welcome, Greg. I'm glad you see what Mandy's challenges are. Diabetes is only one of her many problems. She's got a tremendous fear, almost a phobia, of being fat. She's grieving her father's death. She's worried about her mother's feelings. That's a lot to deal with, don't you think, Greg?"

It was clear he'd gotten the message about names and titles. His left eye twitched each time she called him Greg. Courtney felt a glimmer of hope that they could reach some sort of equilibrium. She wasn't an MD, but she was a doctoral-level professional, board certified in both psychology and diabetes management. This "Courtney vs. Dr. McClure" rubbish had to end if she were going to work successfully at the clinic.

"I'm not sure if we're on a first name basis," Greg said, studying his soiled shirt. "We need to maintain a professional relationship."

"You've been calling me Courtney since you paged me," she said, swirling the ice in her drink. "Does your notion of professionalism only travel one-way? I understand if you want to use titles in the office, but if we're in a bar, we're equals. Correct?"

Greg studied her as he would a specimen under his microscope. His face ran the gamut of emotion, from annoyance to contempt to something else she couldn't define. It drew her to him. He looked almost ravenous, despite his recent feast of Mexican food. She couldn't tell. Or she was just tired, spent from the long day, and imagining things. Probably that.

"I see your point," he said. "Here's the thing. I'm very concerned that the office should be a place that exemplifies the highest standard of care available to patients. They should know, in obvious and subtle ways, that they're in the best hands possible. My father styled himself 'Dr. Eric', which I thought was ridiculous. It sounded like a nursery school, where the kiddies address the teachers as 'Miss First Name'. We're in a serious business, and we need to reflect that."

Nursery school? This man was too much. Maybe it wasn't his arrogance she had been revolted by. Maybe he was deeply doubtful of his ability to lead the clinic. He could be showing classic inferiority-based thinking. It wasn't really her problem, though if she had to work with him, it was. It was a problem not to be solved tonight, that was sure.

"Fine. We'll be 'Doctors' in the office. However, if I hear my first name, yours will be used as well, regardless of the setting." Courtney drained her bourbon, wished for another, but knew she had to leave before she exploded. "I should be getting home.

You can enjoy the rest of your dinner without me. See you tomorrow at work."

As she drove to Miramar Beach, Courtney was appalled at her behavior. She never drank, with the exception of sparkling wine at holiday events; even then she barely finished half a glass of the beverage. Greg had upended her equilibrium, starting with the emergency page and with his constant use of her given name throughout the evening. Then the sight of the hospital, identical to Drew's clinic, had ruined her calm. What an evening. But she had no valid excuse for trying to gain the upper hand with Greg. An oversized ego like his was better left unchallenged, since he was the source of her employment.

Lord, please help me with my own ego. I'm in uncharted waters, and I know I'm still not over Drew. Help me rediscover the calm, cool-headed Courtney I used to be. And thanks for my many blessings – family and friends I love and who want the best for me.

After not one, but two different traffic jams on the Turkey Creek bridge, Greg was finally home. He threw his keys on the entry table. What a night. Mandy was going to be fine, at least until her next steak house binge. Cathy had warmed to Courtney, which was a good thing. Courtney, however, had not warmed to him. What had he done that bothered her so? The name vs. title argument seemed fake. Or maybe he was a bit of a Neanderthal, as one of his many past dates had said.

Neanderthal or not, his responsibility was to make the clinic successful. He had to follow his gut.

His gut told him proper titles were part of helping patients feel secure as they dealt with the complex reality of living with diabetes. Courtney needed to get on board.

She had made a good point, though, about after-hours interactions. And what had possessed him to take her hand when she splashed her drink? Her velvety skin, her delicate fingers, and her slight tremble had caused him to want to both challenge and protect her. She was a woman of secrets, he decided. What caused her to land in Destin? Grief over her parents was a valid issue, but it had been five years. There had to be more than cold weather prompting her escape from Indiana. She needed comfort, and he'd been told he was good at that. A certain kind of comfort, one usually involving physical actions. It hadn't worked tonight.

Even her willingness to stand up to him was appealing. Courtney wouldn't resort to kidding around though. Her reaction to their differences was direct and heated. He had a feeling he was in for some challenging days with her on his staff. The wonder was, he was looking forward to it.

His phone rang, interrupting his continued reverie, which had now focused on Courtney's revealing blue eyes. He could gauge how much trouble he was in by how deep the blue turned. He'd been in a bit of trouble tonight.

Seeing the caller ID, he groaned as he noted three other missed calls, all from Taryn. She was calling to check on him, berate him for not answering earlier, and fish for details about where he'd been. It was sad that he could predict their conversation before anyone spoke.

"Hi, Taryn," he said slowly. "It's been a real day for me. How has yours been?" He hoped in vain to avoid some scolding by getting her to talk about herself. Fingers crossed.

"My day was fine," Taryn said, obviously gritting her teeth. "But no matter how busy you've been, it's rude to ignore my calls. A simple text would be enough for me to know you're okay. Is that so hard?"

"It is hard. I've been at the hospital due to an emergency with a patient."

"Which patient?"

"Taryn, how many times do I have to remind you? I can't talk about my patients. The way you grill me, you'd think I was with someone else."

Clearly sensing an opening, Taryn responded. "Why would you even say that, Greg? Who were you with? Of course, you can't talk about your patients, but my female radar says you're hiding something."

"I'm hiding nothing. I was at the hospital after an emergency page. My new psychologist was also there. The important thing about this evening is the patient got past this crisis and will live to see another day."

"New psychologist? That woman your father hired? I thought you were going to let her go. The clinic budget just won't support her salary. Your words, not mine."

"I know what I said," Greg said with a sigh. "But she's good with patients, and her billings should support her costs. Her office was empty anyway, furnished with old waiting room stuff. She already has a full schedule. She'll be a good addition to our staff."

Taryn did her usual bait and switch. Suddenly she

was sweet and accommodating. "See, you're a great director, Greg. You've already figured out what your dad couldn't, which is how to make the clinic viable. Just remember you're not beholden for a hire you didn't make. That's all I'm saying."

"Fine," Greg said. "I've got to let you go. It's late. I'm tired. Long day tomorrow. Talk to you soon."

"I know when I'm being dismissed, Greg. Talking soon had better mean a phone call from you after work tomorrow. You owe me that." Taryn ended the call before he could reply, typical of her style when she was angry. She always got the last word.

Greg was grateful for the silent phone. How had he and Taryn gotten to this point? They'd had what he thought was a casual friends-with-benefits relationship. Lately it had turned into a game of Taryn's pursuit and him running away. Early on, Taryn had been wonderful, understanding of his work challenges at the clinic and tolerant of the hours he had to work to make the clinic a success. Gradually, he'd realized she wanted more than he did from their relationship. Her conversations became focused on friends who got engaged, how much money their fiancés made, and the best areas in Destin to raise kids. Some men were enticed by such clinginess, but not him. He liked a woman with an independent spirit, one he could engage with in places other than the bedroom.

Like Courtney. They'd just known each other for one day, but his instincts told him she was a woman with passion and intelligence. In a single day he'd seen her bond with patients, argue her views with him *(her new boss, no less!)* and steel herself to walk into a hospital reminiscent of a painful time in her life. Her beauty was an added bonus. He might just consider paging her routinely so he could see her in those tight jeans. She'd never wear them to work, which was a shame.

So much for my emphasis on professionalism at the office. Courtney has me fantasizing about her body. I'm a Neanderthal, all right!

Chapter Three

The first week at the Diabetes Care Clinic was comparable to drinking from a fire hose, but Courtney still enjoyed the pace and the patients. Jackie tried to allow some breathing room in her day, to no avail. Greg had computer access to her daily schedule. He used this to fill Courtney's vacancies with patients from his day, saying they might as well meet the new clinician to help them with motivation, mood, and adherence to their diets. She was sure *Greg's* motivation was to increase her billings, given his concern about being able to cover her salary.

For now, that was fine with her. She relished treating patients of all ages. Some had a new diabetes diagnosis, while others had lived with the disease for many years. She had to admit, though, by the end of the day Friday she was ready for a breather.

Her busy days also meant she hadn't had to interact with Greg much. Their complicated conversation at Crabby's still rattled her. They had a certain sizzle, no doubt about it. His touch had affected her in a way few others had. He seemed to feel it, too. He was avoiding her at the office as much as she was him, which was just as well. Few things were uglier than having a relationship with a boss in a small, gossipy setting. The clinic didn't seem to be a hotbed of chatter, but Courtney knew romances in the workplace brought with them plenty of snide remarks. And those were the romances that ended well!

She remembered Sherry's experience at her accounting firm in Gordon. Sherry was a new grad, full of enthusiasm when her supervisor suggested she play on the firm's softball team that spring. What started as a fun diversion ended with Sherry's resignation due to her boss's harassment during postgame gatherings at the local bar. Thanks be to God Sherry had found Patrick. He was a fine man and the perfect complement to her analytical nature. Patrick made a modest living as a county caseworker, while Sherry earned more than enough as an accountant for the hospital. Social services and numbers-based living worked well in their case.

Courtney was glad for her sister's happy ending, but she was worried she might be repeating Sherry's earlier history if she continued to think about Greg's touch. It was time to focus on other things. She wanted to establish herself in the Destin area, make new friends, and join some local organizations. She'd have a social circle in no time. There would be no need for Greg McClure to muddy the water!

After sleeping in on Saturday, Courtney cleaned her small condominium. She added some bargain finds from the big box store – pillows and small side tables for the living room to complement the old sofa from her apartment in Gordon. Her budget had barely stretched enough to buy a one-bedroom, two bath, oceanfront unit. The two bunk beds in the main hallway allowed her to entertain overnight guests.

It was time to enjoy her "front yard", as she called the white sand beach outside her condo. Destin and neighboring Miramar Beach had more than lived up to her expectations. Unlike back home, her walks here had endless variety. Sometimes she used the boardwalk, crossing the street to browse in the souvenir shops. On the days she ran, she could almost make it to the Destin city limits, able to see the restaurants and boutiques edging the water.

Today she took an afternoon walk and watched the dolphins play in the ocean. Their freedom enthralled her. What would it be like to have no worries? Well, it would be heaven, literally. She wasn't ready for that yet, so she had to keep taking one day at a time. Courtney shrugged and turned toward her unit, using her cell phone to order a pizza as she sank her toes into the sand with each step. It was time for a celebration. She'd made it through her initial week working with Greg, though their avoidance of each other probably wouldn't last. The rest of the staff had been easy. The nurses welcomed her as another female who might stand up to their domineering boss. Jessica, the dietitian, seemed like good friend material, warm, candid, and full of teasing humor. All in all, it had been a positive week.

Hearing the doorbell twenty minutes later, she deftly handled the hot pizza box and tipped the driver. She was about to shut the door when an elderly woman appeared in the hallway.

"Hi, honey," the woman said. "I'm Minnie, from next door. Welcome to Miramar Beach, and to our condo community. I'm the ambassador for this floor, so I'm ready anytime to give you our new resident welcome basket. It's loaded with coupons and goodies from local merchants. The Silver Sands outlet mall has especially good deals."

"Minnie, it's great to meet you," Courtney said, studying the petite, silver-haired woman. Minnie couldn't weigh more than a hundred pounds. Courtney sensed a chance to make another friend, via pizza and soft drinks. "I'm Courtney Bledsoe. Have you eaten? And if not, do you like pizza? I've got plenty for both of us."

"That would be lovely," Minnie said with a raspy cough. Her silk caftan rustled as she caught her breath. "I get so tired of eating alone. My husband has been gone for a year now, but it's still foreign not to ask him what he wants for dinner."

The pair sat at Courtney's small dining table. She transferred pizza slices to plates and added bowls filled with bagged salad she had on hand. "I'm truly sorry about your husband, Minnie," Courtney said. She didn't mention her parents' deaths or Drew, and instead allowed Minnie to tell her story.

"Thanks, honey. Dominic and I were married for fifty-five years, ever since I was a girl of twenty. We had our ups and downs, but we always figured things out. Our two daughters are still up north in Fort Wayne, Indiana. I couldn't take the winter weather anymore, so after being a snowbird for several seasons, I bought my condo here."

"Minnie, we already have a lot in common. I'm a new resident from the north, actually from Gordon. We were practically neighbors before this!"

After swallowing a hot bite of pizza, Courtney continued. "Grief is tough, as you know, Minnie. I'm a psychologist but I still can't prescribe a foolproof way to heal from such loss. It takes the time it takes, which sounds like a huge copout to my patients."

"I'm sure you help a lot of people," Minnie said, aiming a bony finger at Courtney. "My youngest granddaughter sees a therapist for her anxiety. It's been a huge benefit to her."

"I'm glad, Minnie. What did you do before you retired? Were you a stay-at-home mom?"

"Not exactly. My Dominic had his own contracting business. I did the books and reminded him when his expenses were getting close to the bid estimate. Working together had its downside, but I was always flexible for the girls, which was important to both of us."

"I'll bet you watch the home improvement shows and predict all the backstories," Courtney said with a smile. "Those episodes end so neatly, after they've glossed over all the unforeseen glitches that renovation and construction entail."

"Very true," Minnie said, hacking a few times. "Dom lived to see several of those shows, and we always had a good laugh about them. We really liked it when the 'before' pictures were similar to our kitchen or bathrooms, but the host would gut it all. We thought it was pretty wasteful."

"As you can see, my condo was recently redone," Courtney said, pointing to the kitchen with its white Shaker cabinets and quartz countertops. "I got lucky because the owners were divorcing and wanted a quick sale. Not that I relish their split, though. I did have to provide my own furnishings, which as you can tell are still a work in progress. What's your unit like?"

Minnie smiled, an effort that lit up her lined face. "It's this exact same floor plan, Courtney. The only difference is that it's a mirror image of yours. It's not updated, but that's okay with me. I'm very comfortable. And you'll find out quickly that guests from the north tire of the bunk beds. They're a built-in guarantee people won't stay too long!"

Both women laughed, and Minnie changed directions. "What about you, Courtney? You said you're a psychologist. Do you work at one of the mental health centers? Or are you in private practice?"

"Neither," Courtney said with a frown. "I'm at the Diabetes Care Clinic. I'm the first psychologist they've had, and I think I'm on shaky ground. The director has financial concerns. His dad hired me, but Dr. Greg McClure didn't agree with that decision."

"One of my friends from church goes there," Minnie said. "She loves the younger Dr. McClure. He's helped her stabilize her blood sugars which her family doctor hadn't been able to do. You have a good boss."

"He's an expert, for sure," Courtney muttered. "His whole focus is on money, though. According to him, if he can't figure out a way to get insurance providers to pay more promptly, my salary will do the clinic in."

Minnie studied Courtney for a moment. "Honey, my husband used to say, 'when everything is said and done, it all comes goes to money'. Bear in mind, he wasn't a miser or a cheat. He was very generous with me and the girls. And with charities and his church."

"Look at my outfit," she added, pointing to her flowing gown and jeweled sandals. "We got this on a cruise. It was hugely overpriced. But Dominic knew

I loved it. His focus on the bottom line just meant if we didn't watch the money, we'd have no business to run. Maybe Dr. McClure is in that same situation. If the clinic isn't paying for itself, no one will get the diabetes care they need."

"That's a helpful perspective," Courtney said. "Perhaps I was too quick to judge. But his resentment of me still rankles. And when we went out for a bite after my first day, he was a little too affectionate. It's confusing, to say the least. I wonder if I should be looking around for another position."

Almost choking into a tissue, Minnie simply replied, "Hmmmm. You've had quite a week, Courtney."

Following another ragged coughing spell, Minnie went on, "We've just met, but I can tell you're off-balance from more than Dr. McClure's focus on money. Was he abusive? Did he pressure you into something?"

"No, nothing like that," Courtney admitted. "I was unsettled when we went to see a patient in the hospital. The building brought up some tough memories. My parents died in a similar hospital, and the building itself was almost identical to a clinic in Gordon. Then I was pretty brittle about referring the patient to a therapy program better suited to her than our clinic. Greg was trying to calm me down, I guess. He held my hand and told me to relax."

"Oh dear, your parents both died? Here I am talking about my grief after a long happy marriage, and you're lost your parents at such a young age."

"Yes, they died in a car accident. They were hit by a drunk driver who was able to walk away. That's only part of the reason I left Gordon. My boyfriend wasn't a good fit despite our history together. That, plus the constant reminders of Mom and Dad were too much. My sister said I was running away, which is partially true. But I've always wanted to live on the beach, and at thirty-five I decided it was time. I guess I was jolted into a bucket list mentality."

Minnie smiled again, this time with moist eyes and a loving pat on Courtney's shoulder. "You have a lot of guts, Courtney. Pursuing your dream after those losses takes real grit. Good for you."

Courtney was ready to change the subject. She wasn't ready to talk about Drew, which would probably be Minnie's next topic. She was also concerned Minnie had barely had half a slice of pizza and only two sips of her root beer. This woman needed to eat.

"Are you okay, Minnie? Have you had that cough checked out?"

"I'm fine, dear. It's just a seasonal tickle in my throat. Some days are more trouble than others. Thanks for asking."

Well, she shut the door on discussing her health, Courtney thought. *But she's a nice woman and my first neighborhood contact. I'm glad we connected.*

The women enjoyed the greasy mozzarella strings of the pizza while Minnie filled Courtney in on the details of living in the condo complex. She offered several tips: to use the parking garage even though street parking was closer (the intense sun and salt spray could damage the car finish), where to shop for designer clothing at great prices (the thrift store operated by the hospital guild), and why there were so few shells on the beach (likely due to deep underwater sandbars that trapped the shells before they got to shore).

Courtney chuckled and thanked Minnie for her

wisdom. "Wow, you're a wonderful friend, Minnie. Let me know if I can help you in any way. My schedule is basically nine to five, but my evenings and weekends are free." She decided to be direct. "Do you drive, Minnie?"

"Not much, and never at night," the older woman confessed. "I know this area well. I take my time. I plan my weekly outings very carefully, so all my errands are done for the next several days."

"If something comes up, let me know," Courtney said. "Really, Minnie, it's a genuine offer."

At that point, Minnie stood. "I've taken up almost all of your evening. It's been a pleasure, Courtney. You let me know if you need anything also." Refusing Courtney's offer of homemade oatmeal cookies, Minnie headed to her condo.

Shutting the door, Courtney marveled at life's unexpected turns. Who would have guessed she'd find good companionship with an elderly neighbor? Minnie had an almost eerie intuition as well. She'd zeroed in on Greg's behavior at the bar and noted Courtney's discomfort was due to more than simply being a new employee.

Minnie was right. Greg's touch had been unexpected and sensual. He sure knew how to use his hands. I wonder what he'd be like without all the pressure from the clinic. How would it be between us if I was just a woman, not an employee who was strangling his budget?

Saturday was Greg's day to spend with his father. Since his wife's death, Eric was vocal in his appreciation of any time Greg could spare. There was no predicting how things would go, however. Sometimes his dad was upbeat and encouraging about the clinic. Other days, Eric would second guess all of Greg's decisions. Today was shaping up to be a combination of the two extremes.

"Let's get the all-you-can-eat buffet brunch at the clubhouse," Eric said as they wound up nine holes of golf. "I'm starving."

"Sounds good, Dad," Greg said. Breakfast was pleasant enough until Eric asked how the week had gone at the clinic. Before he could catch himself, Greg questioned the wisdom of hiring Courtney. As he should have expected, Eric's jaw tightened.

"What do I have to do to convince you she'll be worth her weight in gold, both to the bottom line and to our patients?" he asked, clutching the edge of the table with both hands. "Between helping people find commitment to their lifestyle restrictions and handling their adjustment and depression, she'll pay for herself in no time. Son, you've got to give her a chance."

"I'm doing just that," Greg said. "I've scheduled her with every patient possible. Her days have been full."

Eric paused, evidently considering his words carefully. "Greg, let's consider what you just said. You're referring patients who may not even be ready for or interested in psychotherapy. They'll be frustrated to the point of never considering therapy again. You're filling Dr. Bledsoe's schedule, so she has no time for paperwork or consulting with other clinicians. Do you think that's wise?"

Hating his father's accurate assessment of his approach, Greg fumed. Why did every little thing he said to Eric come out as inept or stupid?

His goal was always to make the clinic a success, but his father couldn't understand that. If he wasn't able to save the business, patients would be forced to find care elsewhere. And he would look like a bumbling idiot.

Sensing Greg's turmoil, Eric persisted in spite of himself. "Listen, Greg, you're doing a good job. I've heard plenty of complimentary things about you and the staff, and I've only been gone a few weeks! I'm just saying to give Courtney a chance. The next ADA continuing education meeting for diabetes educators is coming up. You and Courtney should go. And Jessica as well, if she can work it in. I'll be there, catching up with my old colleagues. I figure if we have four of us absorbing the latest wisdom, we'll have lots of new strategies for the clinic. I checked the program, and there's a half-day seminar for administrators on dealing with insurance companies. With Medicare so stingy they're practically mandating that hip replacements are out-patient surgeries, we need to learn how to get our diabetes services reimbursed at the highest possible levels."

"Dad, there will be no one to run the place if we do that," Greg said with a resigned smile. "I appreciate your concern, though. You're right. I need to attend to current financial realities. But more to the point, how can we cover the cost of registration, hotel rooms, and food for all of us? Isn't the meeting in New Orleans? Even if we drive, and I'd rather not, it's four hours each way."

Eric grinned like a guilty tween caught playing video games under the covers. "Didn't I tell you about the separate account for professional development? I haven't touched it in the last few years.

I went to meetings on my own dime. I knew I was going to retire and that you'd have use for it. The conference outlay will be covered easily."

Knowing Eric's agenda was more than just attending the conference, Greg pondered his father's plan. Eric had been specific about having Courtney go with them. He'd thrown in Jessica as an afterthought. His dad had a plan, all right. He'd hired Courtney on her merits, but her looks and personality hadn't hurt. Jackie had told him there were several male candidates for the psychologist position. According to Jackie, his dad hadn't given them more than perfunctory interviews. Interesting.

Choosing to keep his theory quiet, Greg decided to appease his father. "Good ideas all around, Dad. And strong work on keeping the professional development account quiet. I'd have used it for daily operations by now. Let's have Jackie make our reservations for the meeting."

As they left the clubhouse, Greg's phone rang. Noting it was Taryn he let the call go to voicemail. Eric saw the caller ID and took note.

"Not going to pick up for the love of your life?" he asked with raised brows. "What's that about?"

"She's not the love of my life," Greg sputtered. "To be honest, I'm not sure we're in it for the long haul."

"Trust your instincts," Eric said, again with that annoying grin. "There are better women out there, believe me. Perhaps right under your nose."

Theory proven, Greg thought. *Dad thinks Courtney is a good match for more than just the clinic. Remembering how much he'd enjoyed holding Courtney's hand, and her slight but curvy form in her after-hours clothing, he had to admit his father might be onto something.*

Taryn's voice was curt and cold when Greg called her back a few hours later. He'd showered, gone through the week's mail, and done several other odd tasks as he put off what would be an unpleasant conversation. It was time. Their relationship had run its course. Taryn's response was telling.

"What do you mean, 'we need to take a break'? It's as if we're always on break, Greg. I call, you ignore me, and I'm left wondering what we have together. When we do talk, you're distracted. That damn clinic is the only thing you think about. There's absolutely no stinking excuse for treating me like this. My friend Pam's husband is a *surgeon*, for God's sake, and they spend more time together than we do."

Taryn's profane language was always a marker for her anger. Greg knew her fury was justified. But he was done. Before he could respond, Taryn continued her attack.

"No one takes a break from me," she said. "It's over. I deserved better from you, Greg. My girl-friends, my mom, and even Steve at work all agree. Don't ever call me again."

"I'm sorry, Taryn. I can't argue with anything you've said. I hope you find a man better suited to you. Take care of yourself."

The call ended with no response from Taryn. Despite the sad finale to their relationship, Greg felt only relief. He'd been unfair to her, expecting nothing but casual intimacy from a woman clearly desiring more. He'd been weak at several levels. He felt God's judgment, but instead of examining his own deficiency, he decided to ignore it for now. He'd do better next time.

Walking outside to his garden patio off the kitchen, Greg speculated about the recent turn of events. *Steve will be good to Taryn. With Taryn taking charge, he'll have no choice. And now I'm a free man. Courtney will be at the conference in New Orleans. I'm going to make sure we enjoy each other in that steamy, romantic Louisiana setting. Thanks, Dad.*

Chapter Four

Another week at the Diabetes Care Clinic had come and gone. Courtney and Jessica decided to celebrate at Crabby's. The Friday special was crawfish stew over rice, on which both women splurged as they got to know each other better. Enjoying their after-dinner coffees, they reviewed the week.

"I'm SOOO glad you're at the clinic," Jessica said. "The atmosphere is much more relaxed, but still professional." She rolled her eyes and grinned at Courtney. "Dr. McClure is very worried about professionalism. You've proven we can chill a little but still be conscientious. Your sense of humor is the best."

Worried she had overstepped, Courtney had to ask, "Jessica, do you think I've been too loose? Greg is uncertain about me already. The last thing I want to do is jeopardize my job."

"Not at all. You have a good balance, Courtney. When he gets pompous or annoyed, your subtle remarks calm him down."

"I hope so," Courtney said. "I respect Greg's work.

And I've been careful not to call him Greg to his face! He does know his stuff, that's for sure. Do you ever mind him contradicting what you've told patients? How do you handle that?"

"I do mind," Jessica said, a little too loudly. "Sometimes he's right, but often he's just nitpicking my input. To paraphrase an old saying, 'there are four ways to do things, one being wrong, one being perfect, and the other two being valid judgment calls'. What about you? His comments in staffing today about a certain patient not losing weight quickly enough really bothered me."

Courtney bristled. Greg's condescending reference to Alice Haig's weight *had* bothered her. Alice was losing between a half and one pound per week. For her age and activity level, that was success. The slow weight loss also increased the odds that the weight would stay off. Greg didn't seem to realize that, which again surprised her. But she needed to be tactful with Jessica.

"Yeah, I felt judged, almost shamed. He didn't have to announce it like that in our weekly meeting. Plenty of his overweight patients aren't losing weight at all. Did you think he was singling us out, or am I being paranoid?"

Jessica nodded. "Yes, I felt he was focusing on our work, and no, you're not being paranoid. But, Courtney, it was obvious he was looking at you the whole time. That was wrong. Are you okay?"

"Not okay and also puzzled. I'm wondering what my next step should be," Courtney said. "Maybe on Monday I'll try to discuss it with him. What would you do in my place?"

Jessica's eyes glinted. "Girl, if he'd done that to me

in staffing, I'd have walked out. Which I'll admit, is not necessarily a good strategy. My temper gets the best of me at times, but there's never any doubt about where I stand. People are fine with my style. But my style isn't yours. How do *you* handle confrontation?"

Courtney squirmed. "Generally, I don't do it that well. As a psychologist, my confrontational style is always geared toward keeping the peace while solving the problem. I'll start with, 'you say this, but you do that.' Then the dialogue begins with most folks." Sipping her coffee gone cold, she continued, "I know that won't work with Greg. He's the type that demands a show of strength, or he'll walk all over me."

Jessica beamed her approval. "Exactly. For your information, that's what I had to do when I started at the clinic. Everyone was loving my work with patients, but not Dr. McClure. To be honest, I actually did walk out of staffing once. Never had to do it again."

After they had paid their server, Jessica kept going, "Courtney, how are you doing otherwise? This has to be a big adjustment, coming from Indiana and everyone you knew there." She looked at Courtney with eyes full of expectation.

Knowing Jessica had her number, Courtney was honest. "I love my condo, the beach, and most of the people I've met here. You especially! I'm missing my sister and, as I think you've guessed, I'm getting over a man. I did everything right with him. Accommodated his professional goals, smoothed over his offenses, played nice with his overbearing father. I even kept him in homemade bread each week! Everything was good until it wasn't. I just couldn't stay in Gordon any longer. It was time to live my life, marriage or not."

"You were married?" Jessica asked. "That's news!"

"Not married, but close. We were colleagues, I'd met the family, we had a referral agreement between my college and his practice, and we'd each said the 'L' word. As I said, I did everything right. But he still dumped me. Suddenly the new young nurse practitioner was his favorite person at Gordon Community College. And she wasn't just his favorite in terms of her referrals to him, though they were plentiful and often unwarranted."

"Men are pigs," Jessica scoffed. "Well, not all of them. More to the point, you say you did everything right, but it didn't work out. It sounds like you're taking the blame for a weak, self-interested guy. Cut it out. Learn from it and give Greg McClure what he's got coming to him."

Drumming her perfectly manicured nails on the table, Jessica rolled on. "I'm not sure that being a good girl, doing what a man wants within reason, and living your own life are mutually exclusive. You can be yourself, Courtney. You can be the peace-maker if that's truly you. A man who doesn't value that is garbage. As for your current boss, he should know the real you as well. You're strong, but not as fiery as I am. Just be strong in the Courtney way. Keep the peace, but let him know you're not going to be silent when he's out of line."

Monday dawned. Courtney hadn't slept well, anxious about what the day would bring. Jessica was right. If she didn't clear the air with Greg, he would continue to put her down. Dressing in a casual, Florida-style skirt suit, she headed into the clinic building.

"Don't you look nice!" Jackie said. "That powder blue is perfect for your skin and hair, Dr. Bledsoe. Already this Monday is looking brighter."

From your lips to God's ears. Here's hoping Greg agrees.

"Thanks, Jackie," she said. "Is Dr. McClure here? I need to touch base with him before the day closes in on us."

"He's in his office, on his second mug of coffee," Jackie said. "I brought him two, in big insulated mugs, when I saw the mood he was in."

Both women smiled, the humor not reaching their eyes. *Well, if I can do this when Greg's in what amounts to a four-coffee morning, I can do anything.* She knocked on his partially open door and let herself in.

"What do you need?" Greg asked, just as grumpy as Jackie had predicted. "I'm doing my chart reviews for the day. I can't be disturbed."

"This won't take long," Courtney said, suddenly full of resolve. "It's about staffing on Friday. You opened the meeting full of sentiment about us being a team and the need to be a strong unit to help our patients."

"So? Do you have a point?"

"After your pretty opening, you singled me out about Alice Haig's slow weight loss. You said nothing about your own patients' struggles. You didn't mention the successes I've had with your most difficult clients."

"I have no idea what you're talking about, Courtney. I didn't single you out. Feeling a little persecuted? There's no reason for that. It's a clinic, Courtney. We staff cases at the end of the week, and all of our patients are reviewed, not just yours."

Filled with even more steely determination, Courtney responded. "Greg, you're doing it again. I'm not some student who needs an education about clinic routine, or who requires good evaluation from you. Alice's weight loss is going well by all standards of practice. You know that."

Greg stood. For a second, Courtney wondered if he was going to push her out of his office and bolt the door. Instead, he took her shoulders, as if to emphasize his point. He looked into her eyes, his manner a combination of anger and something else she couldn't identify.

"I run the staff meetings, Courtney. If your tender ego was offended by my style, you'll either get used to it or leave. Those are your options." His hands continued to hold her, more gently, but still firm.

Jerking away from his hold, Courtney slammed the door shut so no one would hear her next words. "Don't you *ever* touch me again, Greg. Yes, I can leave if needed. It would be a shame for your patients, but I won't be harassed by you. Understood?"

Straightening her jacket, Courtney left the room, giving the door another strong swing. As she walked by Jessica's office, her friend gave her two thumbs up. It was eight-thirty. The week hadn't even begun, and she was deflated. But she knew she'd done what was needed. Greg's response would tell her everything she needed to know.

Dear Lord, thank you for the strength to stand my ground. Help me to know the best next step. I may need to find another place to work, but in all things, Your will be done.

Staring at the closed door to his office, Greg shuddered. He wasn't sure if he was angrier at himself or Courtney. What had possessed him to grab her? He knew better. Employees, even those from small-town Indiana, knew offensive behavior well enough to use the "harassed" word. He had been out of line, for sure. He had no right to hold her like that.

On the other hand, he'd enjoyed it a bit. The heat from her fury had traveled up his arms, causing him to be calmer. He loved touching her. There was chemistry there, just as there had been after they'd seen Mandy Eller at the hospital. Courtney couldn't deny it either. Not that it mattered. She was livid. She might even be looking for another job. Not a good outcome of his yielding to his sudden instinct.

So how could he make things work between them? He needed her at the clinic. The patients loved her. Jackie raved about their comments when they scheduled their next appointments with Courtney. Jessica and the other staff liked her also. The lunchroom was filled with laughter when he walked by. Prior to Courtney's arrival, no one had eaten together. They'd either gone out or had sack lunches in their cars while they listened to music. Was his presence so toxic?

Greg admitted he might also need Courtney in a different way. Just as he'd noticed at their ill-fated time at Crabby's, her willingness to contradict him stirred him up. Of course, Taryn had contradicted him constantly with very different results. He'd just

found Taryn annoying and self-interested. Courtney wasn't like that. Her beliefs were always based
on meeting the needs of their patients. His standing
as her supervisor and owner of the practice had no
bearing on her opinions.

His phone light came on, signaling his first patient was ready for him. With a resolve that surprised him, he promised to be more professional
with Courtney. He could do it.

As fate would have it, the patient was Alice, the
source of the recent conflict in
staffing. "Mrs. Haig, we meet again," he said to
Alice. "I hear your work with Dr. Bledsoe has been
going well. What do you think?"

Seemingly shocked by Greg's praise of both
herself and Courtney, Alice stammered. "Well,
thanks, Dr. McClure. Yes, I think I'm doing better.
Dr. Bledsoe and Jessica, the dietitian, have helped
me identify triggers, food and other things, for my
binges. Then I've learned to make substitutions." She
looked defensive and went on. "I know I'm losing
weight slowly, but I feel much better than when I
started. That should count for something, right?"

"Yes, absolutely," Greg replied. "Your blood sugars are validating what you just said. You don't have
as many fluctuations as before and they're trending
downward. Keep up the good work. Are you going
to see Dr. Bledsoe today?"

"Right after this appointment," Alice said. "I've
got my food records, so Jessica is going to sit in
on the session when we start. Then Courtney, I
mean Dr. Bledsoe, and I will meet for the rest of
the hour talking about other things. She has a way
of motivating me to take care of myself. Between

her coaching and Jessica's lower carb recipes, I've noticed my blood sugar readings are in the normal range. Mostly."

Alice looked even more nervous than when he had entered the room. Were his patients frightened of him? Obviously, Alice didn't want to confide in him, which was fine. Greg knew she was working with Courtney on issues from her past. Difficulties with her adult children, the sad end of her first marriage, and so on. Courtney did a nice job of writing carefully ambiguous chart notes, but he'd gotten the picture when he'd reviewed them. Alice needed a therapeutic ear. And that acceptance was helping her tend to herself and her health. Good work, Courtney.

After Alice left his office, he made a few insurance calls and completed some of his paperwork which was appallingly behind schedule. His accountant had warned him about it; if he were ever audited by insurance carriers, the gaps in patient records would doom him. It was telling he was the only clinician who didn't keep up. He'd always hated the mundane, and chart notes were the worst.

An hour later, Greg was proud of himself. The time Jackie had insisted on scheduling for paperwork had paid off. He'd have to tell her. And he should tell Courtney he was sorry about their argument. Time to be a grown up, as his father had said over the years.

He went to the break room to fortify himself with another coffee, and as God would arrange things, Courtney was there doing the same. Time to man up.

"I'm glad I ran into you, Courtney. I saw Alice Haig before you did. You're doing great work with her. I'm sorry I didn't acknowledge that in Friday's staffing."

Courtney started, spilling half of her coffee on the counter. "Thanks, Greg. I appreciate that." Her eyes looked guarded, her body stiff with tension. After wiping her mess, she left the room and shut her office door.

That did *not* go well. He'd have to keep trying. If a good person like Courtney couldn't look him in the eye when he apologized, he must have done more damage than he thought.

Friday came again, and Courtney was walking her favorite patch of beach after the end of the workday. After Monday's blow up with Greg, she'd managed to interact with him on a purely professional basis as they discussed patients. Not that it had been easy. He was as awkward as she was, but they'd built a tentative truce. Why did it have to be this difficult? Why couldn't she find a job with a kind, accepting supervisor? A person who respected her work and wasn't a testosterone-filled guy like Greg? Her inner whining caused her to laugh, then the waves did their usual work of calming her heartbeat and restoring her faith in God's creation. Surely she would find a way to work with Greg. Or find another job. Whatever it took. Wherever God led her.

Putting in her earbuds, she tapped into her favorite walking music on her phone. A few minutes later, she heard a man's voice call out. Thinking it was a runner yelling, "On your left," she took a few steps to the right. Then she sensed a presence by her side.

This tall, muscled man couldn't be Greg. She'd just left him a few hours ago, thankful to be out of his sight for a merciful few days. What was he doing on her beach? This was her sanctuary! She'd have to get firm again, though she didn't know how exactly she could ban him from a public beach.

Pulling out her earbuds, she heard the last part of his message.

"I thought that was you, Courtney. You must live around here," Greg said, feigning innocence. "Didn't mean to interrupt your walk."

Courtney smiled, happy to catch him in his lies. "Of course you knew I lived around here, Greg. My new employee paperwork gives my exact address. And it's obvious you meant to interrupt my walk. What do you need?"

Greg had the grace to look away. "Yep, you're right. I thought we could talk as people, without the distractions of the office. I figured you were ignoring me until I noticed your earbuds. Look, I've apologized for my behavior in last week's staffing, but I know it didn't mean much to you. I'm sorry and running into you at the beach seemed like a good way to rectify the situation."

Greg gave her a sideways glance, then he continued since she hadn't responded. "I know my apology didn't go far enough. The clinic needs you. You're doing great work with our patients. I've had three people this week ask about seeing you for counseling, based on what they've heard from friends or in the waiting room. And my best source of intel, Jackie, sings your praises all the time. So again, I'm sorry."

Courtney laughed. It was true that Jackie knew everything that went on at the clinic. She'd have to thank the omnipotent office manager on Monday.

But for now, she had to deal with Greg.

"Thanks for all that," Courtney said. "It wasn't necessary to come here on a Friday evening, though. This is my private time. I don't work for you 24/7. I don't want to get into a habit of looking over my shoulder for you every time I'm away from the office. Get it?" She knew she was being obnoxious, but her points were valid. Greg had no right to track her down during her off hours.

Greg looked mortified. "You make it sound like I'm stalking you," he said. "That's unfair. I just want things to be normal between us, as fellow workers in a high-pressure environment. That's all. After today, I'll be sure to walk anywhere but on Miramar Beach."

"Sounds good to me," Courtney said, not willing to concede to his embarrassment. "Since we've cleared that up, we can walk toward your car. Which direction should we head?"

Turning around as she followed Greg, she stumbled in a divot made by a child's digging earlier in the day. Losing her balance briefly, she found herself leaning into Greg's side. *Great, just as I'm setting ground rules! And after I told him to never touch me again!*

Greg ignored her proximity and helped her regain her balance. "Careful, Courtney. These beaches are only smooth at the start of the day. Once families and dogs have been around, you have to watch where you walk."

"Thanks. Good advice. Is that your car?"

"Yes, this is me. Have a good weekend, Courtney."

Greg got in his car, which was a new model, Courtney observed. Her ten-year-old Toyota must have cost a third of Greg's ride. So much for economizing because the clinic was in trouble. This guy was such a hypocrite. He even entered traffic without looking at his blind side. But his car probably had those fancy indicators on the side mirrors. She had a painful memory flash. Drew's car had all the latest gizmos, too. God must be telling her she needed to learn to deal with such frivolous men. He kept throwing them in her life path.

Enjoying the brilliant Saturday morning sun, Courtney made her way to the clinic office, her car full of bags and pillows. She had driven by the clinic once before parking. Greg's car wasn't there. When she was sure he wasn't working on the diminishing but significant stack of paperwork she'd noticed on his desk this week, she pulled into the front lot, turned off the engine, and surveyed the contents of her back-seat area. The slipcovers she'd ordered had arrived. She couldn't wait to disguise the worn upholstery on her loveseat and chairs. Art from her old office, in addition to her framed licenses and credentials, would brighten up the faded color. The art would also serve to hide old nail holes and gashes in the wall. She had debated painting the space herself but didn't feel like risking the time and money if she were to find a job elsewhere. For now, it was time to establish herself as economically as possible at the Diabetes Care Clinic.

After about two hours of stretching fabric, attaching picture hangers, and fluffing pillows, Courtney stepped back into the hallway to get the broad view of her office. It looked fabulous, even to her untrained eye. She snapped a few pictures on her phone to send her friend Annie in Gordon. Annie had cemented her relationship with her husband Ben by decorating his apartment. Courtney laughed. There was no cementing when it came to Greg McClure. She wished she could at least cement her job, but even that was doubtful.

Gathering her trash, she turned toward the waiting area to leave the building. A voice thundered down the space. "Now who's the stalker? If I didn't know better, I'd say you followed me in today, Courtney."

Chapter Five

Greg appraised Courtney's office. He had to admit it looked much better. The furniture was covered with a colorful abstract print material. Coordinating pillows edged each end of the loveseat. The upholstered chairs were a solid color that blended with the print. Tasteful pictures were on three walls, with the fourth highlighting Courtney's diplomas and such. The change was so drastic he felt ashamed as he recalled the shabby furniture and bare walls he'd thought were fine for the new psychologist. But at this point, he wanted to tease Courtney a little.

"After all your ranting about you not working for me seven days a week, here you are, Courtney. If I didn't know better, I'd think you missed me after our sweet talk last night." Her blush confirmed what he already knew. There was significant chemistry between them. And he could tell Courtney was aware of it, too.

To break the tension, he touched the slipcover fabric. "This is nice, but a little thin. Do you think it will wear well with the volume of patients you're seeing?"

"It will do for now," Courtney said. "The fabric has to be thin in order to stretch. I used foam padding over the old upholstery, so it won't snag. It would cost a fortune to have someone cover this furniture properly."

Greg wondered what "for now" meant. Was Courtney implying she would be gone soon? Or did she mean the clinic would be out of business before the furniture showed signs of wear? Either way, he wasn't pleased. Before he could ask, Courtney continued.

"Where's your car? I checked before I parked, to be sure you weren't around. And don't worry about these covers and pillows. Jackie said there was a decorating fund of a hundred dollars for me. I covered the rest of it with my own money."

"A hundred dollars?" Greg asked with false dismay. "That's big money for us. I'll have to give Jackie a warning on Monday. By the way, I parked in back, near the coffee shop. I needed my caffeine fix."

Courtney searched his face, finally getting the joke about the decorating fund. She sighed with relief. "Funny, Greg. I tried to get used to the office as it was, but I was concerned my patients would pick up on the obvious. That psych services weren't that important to the clinic. The old furniture sent that message, don't you think?"

"Maybe. I hadn't thought about it, but you're probably right. I was teasing, Courtney. I'll have Jackie reimburse you for all the money you spent. The office looks great. I appreciate your efforts, and your patients will as well."

Studying him some more, Courtney finally spoke. "So why are you here? Jackie told me you were almost caught up on your paperwork. You should be out enjoying your weekend, Greg."

Smiling inwardly at her repeated and deliberate use of his first name, Greg responded, "I was going to announce this on Monday, but I'll tell you now. My dad had a secret fund for the annual diabetes conference, a fund he never touched. We have enough money to send him, me, you, and Jessica this year. I'm here getting us all registered and making flight arrangements. I thought about having Jackie do it, but she's covered up with scheduling all our new patients."

Courtney dropped the bag of trash she was carrying. "What? We can go to the ADA Clinical Conference? That's terrific, Greg. I've only been to one before, but my brain nearly exploded with all the new information I had to assimilate." She picked up the sack, then asked, "But what about the money? My guess is the clinic could use that fund of your dad's for other things."

"That's what I told Dad, but he pointed out I'd learn a lot about insurance and financial management at the conference. You and Jessica will get the latest on dietary and psychological approaches to patients with diabetes. And he didn't tell me about this, but I discovered Dad is to receive a lifetime achievement award. We should all be there for his celebration." Greg took a breath. "It will be a good investment in our future. I can't let the clinic go under. I won't."

"You won't, Greg," Courtney said softly. "You'll make it a success. I know you will."

She turned and waved goodbye as she hurried down the hallway. He had no time to ask her to lunch or discuss the conference further. Courtney made it clear she thought the clinic was empty when she'd come to decorate. And she was making it clear now that she had no interest in spending any more time with him. But she did have faith in his ability to lead the clinic. This woman was a challenge, one he realized he relished. There would be plenty of time to spend together in New Orleans.

A month later, New Orleans was at its most beautiful. The streets sparkled, flowers were in bloom, and the atmosphere was festive. After a smooth flight, Courtney and Jessica settled into their pretty room. It had all the modern amenities, but with Old World decor and a fantastic view of the city.

"I don't mean to complain," Jessica grumbled, "but I'm going to anyway. What is this? Sleepover camp? We can't have our own rooms? You're a peach, Courtney, but I like my space."

"We're lucky to be here, friend. This is not an inexpensive conference. I'm glad to share a room. If things get too cozy, we can set some ground rules. But I imagine we'll be so busy with seminars and meetings we'll fall right asleep every night."

"True, all that," Jessica said. "I am grateful to be here. Anyway, I'm headed to my dietetics breakout forum. See you for dinner."

Courtney's predictions were accurate. She and Jessica barely saw each other during their busy days, except for dinner. Greg and Eric reconnected with old friends each evening, so Courtney and Jessica were able to relax as they explored all that Bourbon Street had to offer. On the last night of the conference, the gala dinner and awards presentation preceded the celebratory ball.

Courtney came out of the bathroom to Jessica's wolf whistle. "Girl, you've got it going on. What a dress! My little sequined top looks like something from the bargain bin compared to that."

"You look wonderful," Courtney argued. "There's nothing bargain bin about your outfit. Your sparkly top is a good contrast to your velveteen slacks. And this dress is left over from my friend Annie's wedding. I did a scripture reading, so I had to look appropriate. This happened to be on sale, at ninety percent off. I had no choice but to buy it."

"Sure, Courtney. You were forced into that purchase," she said, blowing on her newly polished nails. "Your exposed cleavage and tight fit of that knit fabric practically scream Indiana church wedding."

"It wasn't a traditional wedding," Courtney protested. "Annie is unconventional. She and Ben were married in an outdoor ceremony at Gordon Community College. Well, it was supposed to be outside, but the rain moved it to the college common area. Anyway, I was dressed like the other scripture readers! I wasn't a bridesmaid!"

"Uh huh," Jessica said with a leer. "I've got to learn more about Indiana. My whole perception of that corn-fed state is all wrong. You Midwesterners have way more fun than I realized!"

They made their way to the ballroom and found their table. The men stood, and everyone introduced themselves. Other than the four attendees from the Diabetes Care Clinic, the twelve-top hosted eight people from Atlanta. As the hot food arrived, Jessica resumed her usual commentary.

"Can you believe the menu for this shindig is shrimp and grits?" Jessica marveled. Addressing the table, she announced, "Courtney has had shrimp and grits every night this week. I swear, even if we were at a fast-food place, she'd ask if they had shrimp and grits."

"And it's been wonderful each time," Courtney shot back. "Different, too. I can't believe how many seasoning combinations there are for this dish." Taking a delicate bite of her entree, she swooned. "This one is heaven, believe me. The grits are extra creamy. There's probably a pound of butter in each serving, along with a cup of heavy cream. Yum."

After the dinner plates were cleared, Eric received his career award, not only for his excellent care of diabetes patients, but also for his research. Both Courtney and Jessica were surprised.

As his father made his way to the dais, Courtney poked Greg's arm. "I didn't know your dad did research," she said. "That's really impressive."

"Yeah, he's a hard act to follow," Greg replied. "He's published yearly since the early seventies. That's part of the reason I specialized in endocrinology. He was so devoted to it as his specialty, I came on board with no hesitation."

"You can follow his act easily," Jessica said. "You've got what it takes, Dr. McClure. But you'll make your own way. If not research, then something else." She gave him two thumbs up and a salute, to the general laughter of the table.

Eric returned, proud to show his award and the sizable check included with it. "This is for the clinic, Greg," he said, pointing to the check. "It covers all of our meeting expenses. God works in mysterious ways."

"Yes, He does," Courtney said. "But maybe God

meant for you to enjoy this reward for a lifetime of dedicated service."

Greg looked at her with what might have been tenderness. "Courtney's right, Dad. You deserve some sort of treat."

"I have no idea what I'd spend it on," Eric said. "I've got everything I need."

"Well, I'm glad to help," Jessica said, between bites of the triple-chocolate cake that had just arrived at their places. "You could travel the world, or at least part of it. You could add on to your home. You could buy some trendy new clothes. No offense, Dr. Eric, but your duds could use some freshening up. Trust me, the ladies in your circle notice these things."

The table members laughed again, and Courtney was grateful for Jessica's silliness. The music started at that instant. Greg turned, held out his hand, and commanded, "The first dance is mine, Courtney."

Jessica fulfilled her role with a "Woot, woot!" and the table joined in. Courtney flushed and followed Greg to the dance floor.

"You didn't have to dance with me," she said. "Our truce is about professional behavior, not dancing." Against her better judgment, she settled into Greg's arms. He felt good. Solid, masculine, and almost soothing.

"Our truce also includes professional behavior at a national conference," he replied. "If we didn't dance, the rest of the table would wonder why. Believe me, these medical types gossip with the best of them. It would be all over the southern states that I didn't get along with my new psychologist."

Well, that would be true, Courtney thought. *We don't get along at all.* There was no sense in arguing, though. The music was too good to waste on a sparring match with Greg. His tux fit like it had been tailored for him, and he was an excellent dancer. Who would have guessed?

The song ended, replaced with a disco number. Greg continued to hold Courtney close, moving slowly but in a downbeat rhythm with the new song. Courtney tried to pull away, but Greg held tight.

"We look ridiculous, Greg. If you want to avoid gossip, I'd suggest we get back to the table or dance like everyone else."

"Whatever you'd like," Greg said. He led her back to the table and asked Jessica if she wanted to join him for the set of fast music. The younger woman nearly jumped off her chair in response. The pair were soon a part of the large crowd enjoying the nostalgic songs.

Courtney was shocked to find she envied Jessica. Eventually the music would slow again and Jessica, not her, would be in Greg's arms.

Though he had fun with Jessica as they performed all the eighties' dance moves, Greg's mind was on Courtney. He'd almost escorted her out of the ballroom and right up to his suite when she'd arrived in that inky blue, clingy dress. Jessica had teased her about it, with Courtney reminding her it was from her friend's wedding a couple of years ago. Evidently, they'd already had that conversation in their room. It looked like no bridesmaid dress Greg had ever seen. Surely something that fit that well, and was cut so low, was not appropriate for a wedding. Nonetheless, Greg enjoyed looking at

Courtney every chance he got.

Returning to the table, he decided to make the most of his chance to talk to Courtney alone. Everyone else was either dancing or mingling, this being the last night of the conference. Tomorrow's agenda was for an early morning of administrative meetings. The Destin Diabetes Care folks were catching a plane at eleven o'clock. If all went well, he'd be back in the office tomorrow afternoon, catching up on whatever details Jackie had prioritized for him.

But for now, he wanted to get to know Courtney better. She was smart, beautiful, and headstrong. But she held a heavy pain, and not just from her parents' death. He had to be delicate, which was not his strong suit, but he was determined to find out Courtney's secret.

"Have I told you how great you look?" he asked. "That dress is really something. You Hoosiers dress for weddings like Floridian women dress for a night of clubbing." Okay, so he wasn't exactly being delicate. That dress was impairing his smooth delivery.

Courtney rolled her eyes. "The wedding was informal, Greg. My friend Annie is a free spirit. She wore a Greek-inspired toga type gown, and it suited her perfectly. My mantra is that you should be yourself, and Annie was. Both in her own wedding attire and in what she wanted her attendants and readers to wear."

"That dress would indicate you're also a bit of a free spirit, Courtney. Not that I'm complaining."

"Would it help my cause if I told you it was on sale?" Courtney said softly. "And to be honest, at the time I was seeing a guy who made me feel special, like life was worth dressing up for."

Despite her words, Courtney looked at peace. Maybe this guy was ancient history. But Greg wasn't convinced. "If that guy is no longer around, he's a fool," he said. "Were you together long?"

"A little over a year. He was a doctor, a psychiatrist, in Gordon. But things didn't work out."

"His loss," Greg said. "I think a psychiatrist who didn't appreciate you is in need of his own services. He'd have to be crazy to let you go."

Surprised, Courtney scooted her chair away from Greg's. "Well, not everyone can be a stellar endocrinologist like you. I've been meaning to ask about the conference. Has it been worth it? Did you come away from all your meetings with any fresh ideas to help the clinic?"

Oh, it's been worth it, Greg thought. *If for no other reason than to see you in this dress.*

Catching himself before he said that out loud, he answered, "Yeah, it's been a valuable use of time and money. I've got some thoughts about billing and increasing our efficiency at the clinic." Noting Courtney's look of alarm, he continued. "No, I'm not saying your schedule will be even fuller than it is. I'm talking more about using a new scheduling program so Jackie can coordinate appointments better for our patients. I'm not explaining it well, but it's more of a one-stop shopping focus, instead of having people come in multiple times each month. It will significantly decrease our no-show rate, and if the data are to be believed, it will increase patient satisfaction scores. Insurance companies love those scores. And I didn't only focus on the administrative side. I've learned a lot to help me clinically, too."

"That's impressive, Greg. I'm glad the conference

has been useful. My time has been equally well-spent. I've learned several different approaches to use with patients. Jessica has said the same about her meetings. Lots of cutting-edge information about ways to deal with depression, family dynamics, dietary adherence, and the lack thereof."

Greg thought this was enough talk about work. He wanted to hear more about Dr. Psychiatrist in Gordon. "Back to personal stuff, Courtney. What caused you to end the relationship? I'm assuming you broke up with him, because if he didn't want you, he's an idiot."

He chuckled to lighten the moment. "I'm repeating myself. Sorry."

Courtney smiled, a real smile, full of genuine pleasure. "Thanks for that, Greg. In fact, Drew broke up with me. We'd had some differences for a while, related to our jobs and what I thought was our appropriate and ethical referral agreement. His perspective was different. He found the new campus nurse practitioner more to his liking, both personally and professionally. He had to keep those patients coming to his clinic, and she helped with that. And with other things." She paused, and a flash of pain covered her face. "Plus, his dad didn't like me. So, it's all for the best. Annie says I dodged a bullet, and she would know since she's had several encounters with Drew's dad."

"Well, my dad likes you a lot," Greg said with a grin. "You're growing on me, too." Standing, he held out his hand. "They're playing the last few songs, Courtney. It's time for more dancing."

After the last few dances deep in Greg's arms, they made their way back to their rooms. Greg held her hand until Courtney paused to retrieve her key card from the tiny clutch bag she carried. Greg stood close. Very close. He leaned in, and before she knew what was happening, he kissed her. Appalled at her response, but ignoring cautionary mental alerts, she kissed him back. This had to stop.

"Greg, we can't do this. We're colleagues, honoring a temporary truce at best. You're the one who said the gossip mill is strong at these meetings. What if someone sees us?"

Annoyed, but still able to find humor, Greg replied, "If they see us, they'll get a real show. Courtney, we may be tentative colleagues, but we're attracted to each other. I'm getting the impression you feel it also. You've actually been supportive of my efforts this week. You were kind to my dad, too. Admit it, there's something between us."

"Maybe," Courtney mumbled, fumbling with her door key. "But it's late. You have morning meetings. I'll see you at the airport."

Inside her room before Greg could make his case further, Courtney sighed. Why did men have to be so complicated? Greg McClure was fundamentally a good guy, but she'd had enough of ambitious physicians. Drew was a good man, too, but a weak one. His need to fill his clinic schedule with new patients had overtaken his character. Like Drew, Greg would probably let her go if she wasn't useful to the clinic's bottom line. The instant her billings weren't covering her salary, she'd be job-hunting. Greg wasn't weak, he was just desperate to save his father's clinic. She had to protect herself. Kissing him was wonderful, but dangerous.

Too wound up to sleep as she remembered the touch of his lips and grateful for the empty room, Courtney texted a photo of her and Jessica to Annie Upton. She was always a good sport, willing to listen to Courtney's latest dilemmas. Annie would see the picture in the morning and text a funny reaction. To Courtney's surprise, her phone pinged while she was brushing her teeth.

Annie's text was funny all right, but it gave Courtney a jolt.

What a bombshell you are! I remember that dress! And who's the divine hunk to your right? Hubba, hubba! Courtney had meant to crop out Greg's presence in the photo, but she forgot.

Texting wasn't going to work with this complex conversation. Courtney called Annie, who picked up immediately.

"Hi, buddy," her friend said. "You have lots of explaining to do, Courtney. I'm here with a tub of ice cream and open ears. Ben is in Indy for the week, so I'm all yours."

Courtney detailed her dealings with Greg since she'd started at the clinic. She downplayed their supposed chemistry, but Annie wasn't fooled.

"He likes you, right? And you like him, a lot. I can tell. So how are you talking yourself out of giving him a chance? Comparing him to Drew? He can't be as devious and greedy as Drew. God wouldn't do that to you twice." Annie was kidding, but also on target. She knew Courtney well.

"There are similarities, you've got to admit, Annie. Both Drew and Greg need to make their clinics financially stable. I'm a pawn, yet again."

"Quit whining," Annie said, between licks on her spoon. "You know there's a difference between Greg and Drew. You just told me Greg loves his father, who has given him freedom to run the clinic as he thinks best. Dan Clifton was always second-guessing Drew. And Drew couldn't handle the pressure from his dad."

"You think? I'm still wary of Greg and his focus on money. It's hitting too close to home."

"I disagree. They're two very different men. I've got some news, but I'm not sure now is the time." Annie's tone shifted, from teasing to serious.

"Of course, it's the time," Courtney said. She needed to hear whatever Annie needed to tell her. Her intuition told her she knew what it was. What Drew had done.

"You'll hear soon enough," Annie said. "Leslie, that new NP, the one Drew's been all over to get referrals from, is pregnant. They're getting married next weekend in Vegas, of all places. Dan Clifton is hosting a big local reception for the loving couple next month. College administration is putting on a happy face, but I can tell Dr. King is livid. I mean, they're both consenting adults, but it looks pretty sketchy that the community psychiatrist and his best referral source are that chummy. Chummy being the polite word."

Courtney swallowed. She was shocked, but strangely peaceful at the same time. This brought a finality to her relationship with Drew. He'd betrayed her on several levels, but now she was finished with him. There would be no reconciling, no humble explanations from Drew about his sad mistake in letting her go. She was truly free from all the unrealistic romantic possibilities.

"It's okay, Annie. In a strange way, it's a good thing. I don't have to wonder what could have been anymore. It's done."

"I hope so," Annie said, her tone full of drama. "Once a cheat, always a cheat in my book."

The friends ended their call as Jessica returned to the room from her night of partying on Bourbon Street. Courtney listened to the young woman's account of her exploits with her new friends from across the country. That was the fun of these meetings, connecting with others who shared professional bonds and challenges. She was glad for Jessica, but pleaded exhaustion and turned over in her bed. This had been a long day. Tomorrow she'd be in Destin, ready to head to work after the weekend. Back to reality, whatever that meant in her jumbled life.

Chapter Six

Greg was in his office at seven Monday morning. On Saturday he'd caught up on the to-do list Jackie had left him, mostly insurance details that were quickly finalized. He checked his schedule for today, noting that most of his patients were also scheduled with Courtney. It would be interesting to hear if they pushed back at having to meet with her after their appointments with him. Instead of pleading with God for the success of the new scheduling system, Greg said a fervent prayer of thanks for the chance to ensure the clinic's future.

Mandy Eller and her mother were first on his list. Her labs looked better, as did her vital signs and color. Her mother looked more relaxed, too.

"So, ladies, tell me how things have been going," he said. "You first, Mandy, since you're the one in ultimate charge of your health."

"I'm doing better, I think," Mandy said, with a fond look at her mother. "I've figured out how to manage temptation at work. I chew sugar-free gum until my break, then I do my best to follow my meal plan." She gazed at the crown molding above Greg's head, then shrugged. "Okay, I do cheat some when there's cheesecake left over from the dessert cart. But that's been it, and I haven't messed with my insulin pump."

Greg looked at Mandy's mother for confirmation.

"I agree, Dr. McClure," Cathy said. "Mandy's been honest about her slips. More importantly, her mood is a lot better. My only worry is her constant focus on her weight."

"Well, most girls my age are like that," Mandy deflected. "I mean, look at all the YouTube sites on fitness and weight control. You have to admit, I could use some toning up."

"As long as you don't go overboard," Greg said. "Keep up the good work, and be proud of your efforts, Mandy. I know it's hard."

"So that's it? I get to see Courtney now?"

"Yes, you're scheduled with Dr. Bledsoe next," Greg said, still disliking the informality of first name use at the clinic. "See you two next month."

His day went smoothly, surprisingly so after a week away. As with Mandy Eller, his patients were pleased to be checking in with Courtney after their work with him. Jackie had done some speedy adjustments when he'd emailed her from New Orleans about the new approach. He just hoped Courtney's likeability wasn't getting in the way of her effective treatment. Time would tell.

As Jackie locked the doors at the end of the day, he asked her to come to his office. "What's up, Dr. McClure? What did I forget today?" Her worried expression caused him a pang of guilt.

"Nothing's wrong, Jackie. I wanted to give you

a souvenir from New Orleans. Kind of a thank you for tending to things so well while we were gone." He handed her a gift bag. "I remember you collect Christmas ornaments. When I saw this, it reminded me of you."

Unwrapping the blown glass fleur-de-lis ornament, Jackie actually teared up. "Gosh, thanks, Dr. McClure. This is beautiful." She held the ornament up to catch the light playing through the delicate glass. "I can't believe you thought of me while you were so busy in Louisiana. This means a lot."

"You're very welcome, Jackie. I don't thank you enough for all your hard work." Before he could catch himself, he added, "And when we're alone, please call me Greg. You've known me for so long we don't have to be formal all the time."

Jackie left his office at the same time Courtney was leaving hers. He asked if she had a minute.

"Sure, Greg. What's up?"

"I just wanted to see how your first day back was. Sometimes things are off-kilter after we take time away."

"It was a good day," Courtney replied. She hesitated, then squared her shoulders. "I did want to discuss Mandy Eller, if you've got time. She's doing better, but still very focused on her weight and feelings of being fat and unworthy. I really think she'd get better psych treatment at the eating disorders clinic."

Greg pressed his temple, which had started to throb. Nothing with Courtney was easy. "We've talked about this, Courtney. Mandy is getting the treatment she needs here. Even Cathy was pleased with her progress."

"Actually, I heard more from Cathy about Mandy's focus on her size than I did from Mandy. She didn't argue with her mother, which was telling. Greg, her progress won't last long if her eating disorder isn't addressed."

Greg didn't answer. Courtney continued. Was she interpreting his silence as agreement?

"How about this, then," she said. "I could lead a support group one evening a week for our clients with body image issues. We could charge a minimal fee, and Mandy isn't the only patient I see who would benefit from it. If Mandy doesn't improve, we could revisit the referral to the ED clinic."

"Absolutely not," Greg said. "You're busy enough without leading a group in the evenings. It would bring all sorts of liability issues into play, and you'd have to have someone else in the building with you. I can't afford to pay Jackie or whoever else to stay over." *And I want you to keep your evenings free in case anything develops between us.*

Courtney turned on her heel. "Yes, we've had this conversation before, Greg. Patient care versus cost to the clinic. I'm again reminded where I stand in the pecking order."

As he watched Courtney's back, Greg groaned. Just when he'd thought they had reached a state of mutual respect, she was angry again. And she had no conception about the operation of the clinic. Or of the need to keep patients like Mandy on the active client list.

But what if Mandy could remain his patient and also do a round of treatment elsewhere for her eating disorder? Maybe that was what Courtney had in mind. He had a vague memory that this was what she meant. He'd cut her off so quickly she hadn't had a chance to explain her plan. She'd also left in a huff, which was on her. They couldn't seem to figure out how to communicate like normal professionals. That chemistry thing was getting in their way.

Just as he was packing his briefcase, Courtney appeared in the doorway. "What do you need, Courtney? Is there another patient we need to staff?"

"No, I'm here to apologize," she said, pursing her lips. "I didn't give you enough background on Mandy. Even if you don't want to refer her to the ED program, you need to hear what's going on with her."

Sensing his willingness to listen, Courtney continued. "Mandy's a tough one. She's grieving her dad, worried about her mom, and obsessing about her many perceived defects. In her mind, she's totally lacking because she's a girl with Type 1 diabetes. That impacts her sense of the future. Will she be able to have kids? Will they inherit her illness? The focus on her weight helps her dodge those bigger issues. If she focuses on the bathroom scale, she doesn't have to confront what the future may hold."

Courtney took a deep breath. "Or I could be totally off-base. Maybe there are other things going on in Mandy's life. We know she's being bullied; she's hinted at that a few times. And who knows what her relationship with her father was like? Or if they'd argued before he died? Or if he was her biggest support as she tried to deal with her diabetes? Do you get it, Greg? This kid needs to be in an eating disorders group before she does permanent harm with that insulin pump."

Greg studied Courtney as she finished her speech. "I'm listening. You make good points, Courtney. But don't you delve into those topics in your work with Mandy? Does she really need to be referred out when you're able to treat her?"

"Yes, we've touched on those areas, especially concerning her father," Courtney said. "But inevitably, Mandy circles back to her weight and how fat she feels. I think if she did a round of intensive outpatient treatment at the ED clinic, she'd be better able to continue with me."

"How long is IOP? Could I still monitor her diabetes?"

"Typically, IOP is about twelve weeks. And it would be very important for you to see Mandy during that time. I doubt the eating disorders physician wants total charge of Mandy's medical care. He or she will watch her weight and electrolytes and prescribe psych meds if needed. And of course, you'd consult regularly about her status. What do you think, Greg?"

Greg looked at Courtney's gorgeous face. Her eyes were serious but focused on him, which he liked. She was wearing another sundress today, topped with a crocheted sweater that revealed plenty of skin. What had she just asked him?

Tapping her foot in irritation, she repeated her question. "Well, what do you think, Greg?"

"I think you're making a good case for Mandy to attend IOP. I appreciate your analysis. We've got to do what's best for her." Noting Courtney's widened eyes, he reminded her, "We're on the same side, Dr. Bledsoe. You just had to convince me. Are we good?"

"Sure," Courtney mumbled as she left his office. "Same side. Sure."

Courtney reheated the leftovers from Saturday's carryout meal. She'd been too tired to cook after the hassle of the New Orleans airport and the bumpy ride back to Destin. Jessica was an anxious flyer, never having been subjected to turbulence. Courtney's anticipated nap had instead turned into a couple of hours instructing Jessica on relaxation breathing for the duration of the flight.

For a Monday after being away, today had been smooth. Patients seemed to be glad to see her, and for the most part were working hard on their treatment plans. Even Mandy was trying to manage her mood and diabetes according to medical recommendations. But what about Greg? He'd actually agreed to refer Mandy to the ED clinic. No, today hadn't been good; it had been spectacular.

She wished she could get the image of him in his tuxedo out of her head. It was stuck in her brain, and until she talked it through with someone, it would stay stuck. Annie would only tease, and in her way encourage Courtney to get closer to Greg. She was a fine friend, but Courtney needed a more objective ear. She called her sister, Sherry, hoping she would be available to talk.

"Hey, Sis, what's going on in sunny Destin? Or more correctly, Miramar Beach?" Sherry asked. "You okay?"

"I'm fine. I need to talk to my sister. Is this a good time?"

"I'm free as a bird," Sherry said. "What's on your mind?"

Courtney detailed recent events, being honest about her attraction to Greg and their wonderful dances and kiss at the New Orleans hotel. She also filled her sister in on how excited she felt in Greg's arms when they danced on the final night of the conference. "What am I getting into?" she asked. "Am I repeating my sorry history?"

Sherry was still on the line. Courtney could hear her breathing. But she wasn't responding. "Are you there, Sherry? Hello?"

"I'm here," her sister answered. "Wow, you can fill a week, Courtney." Sherry's attempt at humor was a bit half-hearted. "Actually, I may not be the best person to talk to about Greg," she continued. "Remember my own sorry history with my last boss? My first inclination is to tell you to brush up your resume, because you'll be needing a new job soon. You're in a heap of messy trouble, Court."

Now Courtney was the one doing measured breathing. "You really think so?" she asked. "I remember how awful it was when your boss harassed you, but I don't think it's the same with Greg. I kissed him back, after all. And I sure didn't decline his second invitation to dance. I'm not feeling pressured, just worried that our professional differences will kill what could be a positive relationship."

"Maybe," Sherry said. "Okay, we'll acknowledge that the attraction is mutual. Very mutual. But what about his focus on money? Doesn't that sound a lot like Drew?"

"I've given that some thought. On the surface, the situations look similar. But Greg isn't under his dad's thumb like Drew was. Greg just wants to keep the clinic running. That makes me expendable, though. They did fine without a psychologist before I came."

"Maybe they didn't know what they didn't know,"

Sherry said. "My guess is that patients like you and are responding to treatment with you. Greg's got to understand that. He will eventually realize your value to his patients and to his clinic. He's smart, right? He'll get it sooner or later."

When Courtney didn't respond, Sherry continued. "I was too quick to say you should start job hunting," she said. "As I look at the situation, I wonder if you're looking for a quick escape from getting hurt again. Am I being unfair?"

"Yes, you are!" Courtney exploded. "Why would I want to look for a job in a city I barely know?" She paused and reminded herself her sister loved her. "I'm sorry, Sherry. Maybe you've got a point. I'll think about it. I guess I was expecting you to agree, given what you'd been through on your old job."

"And I did agree at first. But this is different, which you said yourself. You're attracted to Greg, and you're dancing with him and kissing him. Believe me, I did none of that with my creepy boss."

Courtney snorted in disgust as she ended the call with Sherry. She was more muddled than ever. Nothing Sherry had said was helpful. She'd started by saying Courtney should look for a new job and ended by agreeing that Courtney and Greg had the hots for each other. No help at all.

Her doorbell rang, and Courtney saw Minnie through the door's peephole. At least talking to Minnie wouldn't be as frustrating as dealing with Sherry. Or Greg. "Hi, neighbor," she said. "It's good to see you again."

"Can you spare time for a visit?" Minnie asked.

Minnie looked better than at their first encounter, and she didn't seem to be squelching the urge to cough. Courtney smiled and said, "Your timing is perfect, Minnie. I just finished leftovers, so I was about to get the ice cream out for a treat. Want some?"

"None for me, thanks. I just wanted to see how you were doing, being that you're a transplant from chilly Indiana. Weather's better here, isn't it?" The women settled in on Courtney's sofa, and Minnie accepted a cup of tea.

"It's nice in Indiana at this time of year, too, Minnie. But I'll admit I won't miss winter at all. It barely gets chilly here, right?"

"Correct. In about six weeks, you'll be adjusted to our heat and humidity, but again, Indiana has those weather patterns, too. So, how's the job, and your boss? You were pretty concerned you might have made a mistake moving here."

The older woman was sharp, Courtney admitted. She might as well be honest. "I love the job. Greg is still a puzzle. We're attracted to each other, Minnie. No sense in denying it. We just got back from a meeting in New Orleans, and I'll admit I was taken by him when we danced."

Pausing, Courtney continued after a few seconds, "The thing is, we disagree on some fundamental things. He's still obsessed with the bottom line, to the detriment of one particular patient, in my opinion. But I may have gotten through to him. We'll see, I guess."

Minnie's eyes twinkled. "I understand. There's nothing more frustrating than being with someone who could be Mr. Right, and knowing you'll fuss and fight much of the time if you're together. Is that it?"

"Mr. Right is not Greg McClure!" Courtney fumed. Grinning, she added, "Perhaps he's Mr. Right-Now."

The women laughed, but Minnie grew serious. "Money's a tough issue, isn't it? Maybe it would help to look at his values. I told you he's a good doctor, based on what my friends have said. What other characteristics have you observed?

Minnie was doing a fine job of counseling, Courtney said to herself. Empathizing and asking leading questions. She was a pro.

"Well, he's a loyal son. A good employer, overall. And he's honest. He'd never resort to over-billing insurance or anything like that. And he can be funny, when he's not all worked up."

"Those are good qualities in a person. And in a man. Is he a looker?"

Courtney laughed again. "Okay, Minnie. You've nailed me. He's quite a nice-looking man. When we danced in New Orleans, it was magic." Why not be honest, she figured. Minnie had a lot of innate wisdom. She could use some.

"Magic, huh? I'm betting you don't use that word often, Courtney. You really like him, and he likes you, I'm certain. What about your concerns related to job security? Wouldn't he keep you around if you two are magic together?"

"No, I'm certain he would do whatever it took to save his clinic. He'd be supportive, write me a letter of recommendation, but he'd cut me if needed. It could even be a better option for him. If I weren't his employee, we wouldn't argue about treatment plans."

"He wouldn't be cutting *you*, just your role," Minnie countered. "Didn't you say his father hired you? Greg had concerns about the psychologist position before you came on the scene."

"All true. So, should I look for another job?"

"Not yet," Minnie said, looking thoughtful. "But you never know. Don't you young people touch base all the time? Network with social media and meet for drinks, even if you're not looking around? You could do some of that, I'm sure."

"Good idea. I'll update my professional profiles, be more active on my psychology listservs, and join the state psychological association. It wouldn't hurt to meet more people anyway."

Aware she'd been talking only about herself, Courtney touched Minnie's hand. "I should apologize. You came for a visit, not to be my therapist, though you're pretty good at it. What's new with you? And with your daughters and grandkids?"

Minnie described the latest with her family. Courtney noticed that the more she talked, the raspier her voice became. The coughing returned, and Minnie drained her teacup.

"I'd better be heading back," Minnie said. "When my cough acts up, it's time for my inhaler."

Courtney made sure Minnie was safe in her condo and returned to her home. That cough was suspect. It was like no allergies she'd ever encountered. Her new friend was seriously ill.

She spent the rest of the evening updating her computer presence. By bedtime, the cyber world was aware of her latest credentials, that she was living in Florida, and conversant with the issues present in patients with diabetes, mood disorders, and eating disorders. After adding several connection requests to her profiles, she joined the Florida Psychological Association. And Eureka! The FPA state meeting was next weekend; she would be sure to attend.

Minnie's counsel yielded a sense of hope, which was the hallmark of a good counselor. That woman had been wasted as an office manager. Thinking of Jackie, though, she realized people in that role had to be therapists of a sort, or else quit in defeat.

As she left for the clinic the next morning, her phone pinged with a message. Courtney skimmed the new connection acceptances before she noticed a message from a woman she'd never met. She clicked on the woman's profile, which listed her place of employment as the eating disorders clinic she was trying to get Mandy enrolled in. Life was taking an interesting turn!

Chapter Seven

Was it only Tuesday? Conferences always left Greg off-center. Of course, he'd been thinking about dancing with Courtney during most of his free time, so it made sense he was iffy about what day it was. Okay, so it was Tuesday. He checked his schedule and was pleased Jackie was learning the new scheduling program quickly. Each of his patients for the day had at least one other appointment with a staff member. It was good for the patients, because it saved them multiple trips to the office. And good for his bottom line, since no-shows would be reduced. He was even more impressed with Jackie's scheduling when he observed that the clinicians still had time for paperwork and chart notes. Nice work, Jackie.

At noon, he walked by the break room, hearing the usual laughter and Courtney's voice. He'd wondered if his staff members were afraid of him. No, they weren't afraid, just stifled by his presence. Or maybe they just didn't like him. He'd work on that.

"Hey, everyone," he said as he entered the room with his bagged lunch. "Have room for one more?"

His query was greeted with a beat of silence, then Courtney responded. "Sure, Greg. Pull up a chair. We were just talking about our worst culinary failures. Jessica denies having any, which I know is a lie. I just confessed to the worst homemade macaroni and cheese ever. My sauce wouldn't thicken, then I burned it by turning the heating element up too high. And I was serving my old flame's parents! It didn't help my case at all, as my presence in Destin will testify!"

More laughter was heard. Jessica interrupted, "So, it's your turn, Dr. McClure. You've had a few bites of your horrendous, no protein, mega-veggie sandwich, so spill. What's the worst thing you've ever made?"

Ten eyes focused on Greg. He cleared his throat. "I was making dinner for a female friend. She's no longer in my life, as Jackie will confirm."

"Good thing," Jackie said in a stage whisper all could hear. "She was a stinker, if you're talking about who I think you are."

"Yes, unfortunately, I am. Anyway, I planned a simple dinner. Salmon, baked potatoes, salad. Dessert was a six-layer carrot cake I bought from a restaurant on the way home from work. Everything turned out perfectly."

"So, what's the failure?" Jessica demanded. "I'd eat all that."

"You would. But I bet you're not allergic to seafood. Turned out the lady I'd been seeing for several months was. She was enraged I didn't know that. Evidently, she'd told me several times when we went out to eat. I honestly didn't remember."

His disclosure was met with a brief silence. Then the five women erupted in loud laughter. Trying to be kind, Courtney tried to stop the upcoming ridicule Greg was sure to endure.

"That could have happened to anyone," she said. "I'm sure your conversations didn't center on food. Easy to forget, right ladies?"

Always the pillar of honesty, Jessica wouldn't have it. "No, Courtney, I'm not buying that at all. We live on the ocean, for Pete's sake. Every good restaurant around here specializes in seafood. You dropped the ball, Dr. McClure."

Laughing at himself, Greg agreed. "Yes, I did. That dinner was the beginning of the end. But you have to credit me for being honest."

He smiled at the loyal contingent of employees. Admitting he was fortunate to have them, he had one last piece of lunchtime business. "While we're all together and not scrambling to serve our patients, I wanted to thank Jackie for her work with the new scheduling system. We're barely back from New Orleans, and she's already using it like a pro. Jackie, you're the best."

Jackie actually got tearful, nodding her appreciation. The others looked on with open mouths, clearly astonished at his generous praise. Greg had his question answered. His staff didn't like him much.

Courtney returned to her office. After a busy afternoon, she settled in for the last hour of her day. Chart notes and a few insurance calls were summarily dealt with. When her phone rang, she hesitated to believe her luck; usually insurance carriers waited a few days before returning her calls.

"This is Dr. Bledsoe," she said.

"Dr. Bledsoe, this is Dr. Cynthia Patterson from

the Destin Eating Disorders Program. Please call me Cindy. Anyway, I just received a referral from Dr. McClure for Mandy Eller. Since you're the psychologist treating her, I wanted to touch base. I'll be faxing a records request after we talk. Is this a good time?"

Greg had referred Mandy? Was the world coming to an end? Courtney forced herself back into professional mode. "Sure, Cindy, this is a good time. And please call me Courtney."

The next several minutes were spent discussing Mandy's complicated history. As

Courtney listened to Cindy, she was both impressed with the woman's expertise and glad she'd pressured Greg into making the referral. He should have told her ahead of time, in fact, she should have made the referral, not him. But she'd educate him about that another time. The important thing was Mandy would be getting the treatment she needed.

After the details of Mandy's condition were summarized, Cindy changed gears. "You're new to Florida, right Courtney? What led you to Destin?"

Courtney decided to be open. "It was a combination of intolerance to cold winters and a failed relationship, Cindy. He was a doctor who relied on my psych referrals more than he cared for me."

"I'm sorry to hear that but glad you're here with us," Cindy replied. "Some men are too involved in their professions to truly care for a woman."

"He's absolutely over-involved in his profession. He's a good man but flawed in that way. Thanks for reaching out, Cindy." Courtney decided to take a risk. "Maybe we can have dinner sometime."

"I'd love that, Courtney. My evenings have been

empty since my son went to college. My ex flew the coop long ago, so I'm free most of the time."

The women set a time for dinner the following week. Courtney hung up and found Greg standing in her doorway.

"I sure hope you weren't talking about me," he muttered. "I don't think I'm over-involved in my professional life."

"You know better, Greg. I was talking about Drew. So, what do you need?"

"I wanted to tell you I referred Mandy to the ED clinic. Were you talking to Dr. Patterson?"

"The very same," Courtney replied. "We're going to have dinner next week. She sounds like a good person."

"I got that impression, too. Speaking of dinner, any chance of us getting together soon?"

Courtney hesitated. Why not go for it and see where her feelings for Greg led? "That sounds okay."

"You're not sounding too enthusiastic," Greg said. "In my opinion, we owe it to ourselves to see if our connection in New Orleans was real. What's your concern?"

"My concern is obviously what it's always been," Courtney said. "That getting involved with a co-worker is risky. No, wait, not a coworker, my boss! I'm feeling vulnerable, Greg."

"All I can say is that I'm not going to take advantage or punish you if things between us don't work out. Those words sound hollow, I know. But there's no way to prove I'm sincere. You're going to have to trust me, Courtney."

Greg's eyes were pleading, a rarity for him. He was right. Courtney would have to trust him. "Fair enough. I'm up for dinner whenever you are." She smiled, and when Greg looked painfully relieved, she laughed.

Ignoring her enjoyment of his worry, he upped the ante. "How about now? It's after six. Neither of us has eaten. Let's head out for a relaxing evening."

This had appeal, Courtney thought. She had her own car, so she could end the evening early. And tomorrow was Wednesday, a busy day at the clinic, and restaurant leftovers would be welcome after work. They arranged to meet at Crabby's, the scene of their first disastrous meal together.

Greg had to admit this was much better than their first outing at Crabby's. He understood Courtney better now. Her relationship with Drew had left its mark. He also respected her expertise as a psychologist, having seen her work up close. But one thing hadn't changed. She was still devastatingly sexy, even in her casual top and slacks. That figure of hers refused to be hidden, even under office attire.

They were munching on appetizers, which he was thankful he didn't spill all over his shirt, when his phone and pager went off simultaneously. Answering the phone, he was surprised to hear Jackie's voice.

"Dr. McClure, it's Jackie. I'm still at work and got a call from the hospital. Your dad's been admitted, and they were trying to find you. Evidently, he's stable, but he had a heart episode." Jackie's voice held a slight tremor. Greg knew it was serious.

"Thanks, Jackie. Get yourself home; it's too late for you to be at work. I'll call when I know more about Dad."

Courtney had picked up the gist of the conversation and stood as Greg did. "Do you mind if I go with you to the hospital?" she asked.

"Actually, I'd appreciate it. I have no idea what a 'heart episode' refers to. I'd like your support, if you've got time."

Courtney patted his shoulder. "Consider yourself supported. Let's go."

The drive took under ten minutes. Once at the emergency department, Greg was taken to see Eric. The older man smiled when he saw his son.

"Relax, Greg. I'm fine. Turns out I'm a candidate for a pacemaker, though. I'll be out of here tomorrow. This getting old stuff is a real pain. But thanks be to God, it's an easy fix."

Knowing his father was minimizing his anxiety, Greg played along. "Yeah, you interrupted a nice dinner, Dad."

"Not with Taryn, I hope." Eric's eyes narrowed with concern. "Not that it's any of my business."

Greg chuckled. "Why should now be any different? You've always been in my business. But I told you Taryn was out of the picture. Let me bring my date in." He left, walked down the hallway and waved Courtney in.

When Eric saw her, his face relaxed. "Dr. Bledsoe, it's a pleasure to see you. How have you been settling in with my cranky son? He can be a handful. Of course, you seemed to have the upper hand in New Orleans."

"I'm not sure about that, Eric. But Greg has a few redeeming qualities. More importantly, I'm glad to hear you're going to be okay after this little detour into cardiac care. Anything I can do?"

"No, nothing," Eric said. "Maybe one thing. Get out of here and finish your dinner with my son. You both look tired and hungry. Don't work so hard, hear me? The clinic will be fine. It's weathered all kinds of health care changes and payment systems. Trust me." He shooed them out of his room and after consulting with the emergency physician, Greg turned to Courtney.

"I suppose we should follow orders and eat," he said, eyes brimming. "I'll admit, I was scared."

"Who wouldn't be?" Courtney said. "If you want to drop me at my car in Crabby's lot, we can call it an evening. I'll have cereal or leftovers at my house."

"No, I want to have a real dinner, Courtney. Please." Greg paused, then continued. "To use your jargon, I need to process."

Courtney nodded. "I agree. We both need to talk about the fright we just had. Crabby's it is."

Greg found himself telling Courtney about his convoluted relationship with Eric. His closeness with his dad had always included a measure of competition. How could he live up to such a successful man's legacy? When his mother was alive, she buffered their spats. Now there was no one to fill that role. He wondered if Eric had retired because of that. Had he wanted to give Greg a clear playing field at the clinic? What did that say about his love for his father? Was he so driven that he'd made his father uncomfortable in his own professional home?

As he talked, Courtney began to shake her head. She finally interrupted his guilt-laden spiel. "Quit it, Greg. I had no idea you were so filled with remorse about your father. I don't quite understand it. All sons want to measure up to their dads. You love

Eric so much. Your mother knew that. And I've seen changes in you. You're more open with him, less intent on being better than him professionally. You were genuinely proud of his award in New Orleans. I think this evening has frightened you so much that you're taking on a villain's role to make sense of it. There's really no need for that, none at all."

Greg looked at the complex woman across the table. "Thanks, Courtney. I needed to hear that. I'm not sure I agree with your charitable take on things between me and my father, but you make some good psychological points."

They both chortled and dug into their cups of gumbo. Courtney put her spoon down and kept talking.

"We should also talk about the elephant in the room. What if the clinic does stumble? With payor systems changing the rules almost daily, things could go south fast. Through no fault of yours, I might add. You have to be ready for hard times, with the belief that they won't be due to your management or deficits. Your dad has even mentioned the clinic's troubled years. Right?"

"I guess so," Greg conceded. "I'd still think any failure was my doing, though. And if worse came to worse, what if I need to cut back?" He looked at Courtney; she understood immediately.

"If the role of psychologist needs to be made part-time or eliminated, I'd understand. Maybe it would be for the best. We could be a normal couple, without workplace drama interfering." Courtney tilted her head, gazing at Greg.

"God forbid," Greg said. Lightening the somber mood, he added, "I kind of like the workplace drama.

Look at how well things went in the lunchroom."
Grinning, he continued. "My terrible relationship
skills were the talk of the staff. Plenty of drama there."

"I think it was more comedy than drama," Courtney noted.

After their meal, Greg walked Courtney to her
car. Deciding the opportunity couldn't be wasted,
he hugged her, then cradled her face in his hands.
"Thanks again for tonight, Courtney. It was some
weird date, huh? A hospital visit, and a discussion of
the clinic's demise. Can I romance a woman or what?"

Courtney didn't reply. She lifted up on her toes
and kissed Greg, with more than a little passion.
Wow, he'd have to be discouraged more often, if
that's what Courtney liked. After the kiss, he took
the big risk.

"Can I come by your place? It's still early, despite
all we've packed into this evening. What do you
say, Courtney?"

Kissing him again, she shook her head. "No, I'm
exhausted. And I want to check on my neighbor.
She's a frail old lady, but we're friends. As I recall,
you cautioned me about older folks taking advantage of me, but it's not like that. She's actually been
quite a good counselor concerning my love life."
She smiled and got in her car, peeping the horn as
she pulled away.

"Great," Greg said aloud to himself as he unlocked
his car. "An elder is giving Courtney romance advice. Maybe we'll be allowed to hold hands soon."

Courtney worked nonstop the next day. Despite
Jackie's efforts to clear an hour for daily paperwork,

this was one of those weeks when half her clients were in crisis. Some crises just involved the need to talk through an upsetting event with an objective listener. However, one patient's depression had worsened to the point he was questioning the need to live. After a draining session and a thorough suicide assessment, he was on his way to his brother's home so he wouldn't be alone. A follow-up appointment had been set for later in the week. Courtney was grateful the clinic doors had been locked for the day. She was empty, physically and mentally.

Trying to type her case note, she heard Greg speaking to Jackie in his office. Though she couldn't hear every word, Greg was asking Jackie if his father had ever had to cut staff hours. Loyal clinic historian that she was, Jackie admitted Eric had scaled back payroll by fifteen percent one year, not laying anyone off, but trimming everyone's paychecks. Two nurses had quit, saying they just couldn't support their families on that wage, which was understandable. Jackie emphasized the cut had only lasted three months, with Eric managing to economize in other areas to get through the lean period. Greg's only reply was a weak, "Thanks, Jackie. Have a good evening."

Well, this was a suitable end to a difficult day. Maybe Greg had been dropping major hints at dinner last night. Hinting she was expendable, or at least in line for a salary reduction. She couldn't be angry. Greg had been worried about his father, the clinic, and most of all, not measuring up to the impossible standard he'd set for himself as clinic director. Maybe he'd been trying to protect her by implying she should start looking around. Minnie had been right. Greg would be reducing the psychologist *role*, not her. He did seem to care for her. He'd wanted to come over after dinner. But she still had a mortgage to pay, and she had to protect herself. She knew she could find a job in Indiana immediately, but she loved living in Destin. Time for action.

Dialing her phone, she connected with Cindy Patterson on the first ring. "Hello, Courtney. Judging by the caller ID, I'd say we're both working a long one today. What's up?"

"I've been thinking, Cindy. The clinic here is changing, and I may be open to other professional options. Would you let me know of any jobs you hear about? Since I'm new to the Destin area I'll probably miss opportunities that you might be aware of."

Cindy paused and Courtney could hear her pulling up an email. "The state psychological association's job board is updated daily, Courtney. Check on that first. What kind of job interests you? Do you want to stick with patients with diabetes?"

"I'm a generalist, Cindy. And I'm adaptable. The job postings will tell me a lot about fit. Thanks for that tip."

"You're very welcome. Any interest in eating disorders? We're always on the scout for psychologists. It's a tough population to treat. People get burned out fast."

Courtney took a second to think about Cindy's question. "To be honest, I wouldn't want to work full-time with those patients, for the reason you just mentioned. I'd be burned out fast. If you ever have part-time options, let me know." Courtney laughed at herself and went on. "Honestly, Cindy, I like food too much! My big plans for tonight include baking several loaves of cinnamon-raisin bread to send home for Memorial Day."

Cindy assured Courtney that a love of food wasn't a hindrance to the job and the conversation ended on a positive note. Courtney resolved to make checking the state job board one of her evening rituals.

At home, Courtney kneaded the first batch of dough. Her thoughts soon consumed her; she needed a new job, and fast. Greg liked her well enough, but his clinic was struggling. Drew was married, so returning to Gordon would be out of the question. She was a chicken, she admitted, but seeing the happy couple on a regular basis was more than she could take. Plus, she loved the Destin area. Working the dough, she knew for certain she didn't want to go back to her former hometown. She professed to be a woman of faith. God would guide her.

Looking down, she groaned at the thready dough on her countertop. She'd kneaded it way too long. Thankfully, she hadn't added seasoning or raisins yet. This loaf would be reserved for French toast or croutons. Well, there were worse things.

More focused now, she quickly had three properly kneaded loaves in the oven. As she sipped an iced tea, her phone rang. The caller ID revealed Cindy Patterson's name.

"Cindy, how are you?" she asked. "I'm surprised to hear from you so soon. Is everything all right?"

"Things are fine," Cindy replied. "I wanted to check with my hospital administrator before I talked to you further. We've been thinking about a joint position with a few of the colleges in the area. The psychologist would travel between the college sites, doing outreach and psychoeducation programs. The role wouldn't be focused on eating disorders, but more on stress management, dealing with demanding courses of study, and especially on the challenges of nontraditional students. If there were students who needed referrals that the colleges couldn't handle, you could direct them to our system. And the referrals I'm talking about could be to any of the programs the hospital has. Eating disorders, obviously, but also mood disorders, anger management, and so on. We've had several applicants just out of their degree programs, but until you popped up, no one had any seasoning or life experience." Cindy laughed at herself. "I'm making you sound practically geriatric! I just mean you have some background treating all types of patients. And with your work at GCC, I know you'd be a good fit with most categories of students. What do you think?"

"I think I'm intrigued," Courtney said. "My initial impression is really positive. What proportion of time would the eating disorders part be?"

"Just the IOP. We have trouble staffing that, since it takes three hours each evening for three days a week. Our clinicians are covered up doing individual therapy. An IOP position also gives patients a chance to hear from a different clinician, so they eventually realize the message is consistent – food can be their joy and strength, not their enemy."

Deciding to take a risk, and to trust the guidance from God she was always spouting, Courtney plunged in. "What would my next step be, Cindy? I'll shoot you my resume after we end this call. What else?"

Cindy detailed the interview process, which was much less demanding than what the Diabetes Care Clinic had subjected Courtney to. Arrangements were made for Courtney to ask for a half day off from the clinic so that she could meet Cindy's staff. After that, Cindy would let her know the decision within a week.

Hitting the end button, Courtney shook her head. Her old feelings of being a coward and a quitter resurfaced. She'd quit her life in Gordon after Drew ended things. Now she would be leaving Greg's clinic when things got tight. But wouldn't that be good in the long run? He wouldn't have to keep her on out of guilt or obligation. She could explore his personality with no fear of setting off her boss's temper. And he could do the same, without worrying he was crossing the line with an employee. Greg would see that it was a win-win, right?

Pulling the three loaves of bread out of the oven, Courtney wondered if she were developing a bad habit, one where she was a runner, a person who left difficult situations rather than seeing them through. At what point did following your bucket list turn into being a big coward? How did tending to your own needs balance with having the guts to stay in a difficult environment? Since none of these questions had immediate answers, Courtney cleaned the kitchen and went to bed.

Chapter Eight

Still tired from a restless night, Courtney was happy her schedule was more manageable than yesterday's. Jessica popped her head into Courtney's office and asked, "What are your plans for lunch, Court? I see we both have two hours free, and since that happens, uh, *never*, I thought we should escape for a meal that wasn't in baggies. Want to come?"

"Sounds great, Jessica. Come get me when you're ready to go."

The morning flew by. The patient with suicidal ideation called in as promised. He reported feeling better, and since his brother was also on speakerphone, Courtney felt encouraged. Other patients were a mix of successes and struggles. This was the life of a healthcare worker, she thought. Each day was different. You had to be focused, but aware that some things were out of your control. You did your best and trusted God.

At the restaurant, the two coworkers settled in. After ordering, Jessica took the floor. "So, how are you, Courtney? Do you need a friendly ear? You've been down lately, I think. Sometimes you're up, though. Dr. McClure seems to impact your mood." She looked at her napkin and added, "I know I'm not a psychologist, but I think I'm a friend. You okay?"

Surprised by her coworker's accurate take on her situation, Courtney nodded. "Thanks for your kindness, Jessica. I trust you, so I'm going to be honest. Greg and I have something between us, but I'm not sure it will survive being coworkers. Maybe I should be working somewhere else."

Jessica shrugged. "I get what you're saying. Jackie has been looking glum. The nurses say that's a sign things aren't going well in the finance area." Studying Courtney, she smiled. "The thing you've got going for you is that psychologists are more employable than dietitians. I'm going to stick it out at the clinic. But if you can find something else, maybe it would help you on both fronts – a stable job and a chance to dance with Greg when you're not at a conference."

Courtney laughed. "My poker face needs some work, huh? You've nailed it, Jessica. It's just so scary. I've adjusted to being in Florida, but now I'll probably have to adjust to a new job. Maybe the payoff with Greg would be worth it, if he can understand my rationale."

"Isn't that what life's about? Taking chances and seeing what's in store? It's really exciting to wonder what the next chapter will bring."

Thinking about her parents' deaths and Drew's betrayal, Courtney shuddered. "My experience has been different. Life's 'next chapters' haven't been so good for me. I escaped Indiana, but at what cost? My sister and old friends are there. Maybe I lack the courage life requires."

"Nope, you're wrong," Jessica said as she sipped her soda. "It took lots of courage to uproot your life and move here. You were trusting life could be better, but you saw no point in staying in a place filled with sad memories. Your sister is about to start her new life, and you'll be able to see her plenty. She'll visit here and you'll go back to Gordon. But for now, you've got to decide what's worth fighting for. And despite all my frustrations with Dr. McClure, he's a battle you should engage in. You two have a real thing, believe me."

The week finished on a calmer note at the clinic. Patients were working hard, staff members were able to tend to paperwork in a timely fashion, and Greg seemed encouraged that his father was doing well at home with the help of a caregiver. Courtney was glad to hear Greg's news.

"Yes, Dad is doing well," he told her after the clinic had been locked up for the week. "I'll be with him tomorrow for most of the day. No golf, unfortunately. I'm not sure how we'll pass the time, but maybe some quiet conversation will be good for both of us."

"I agree," Courtney said. "You two need to talk, and not about which new putter is the best. You're both ready."

Greg smiled. "That said, I'm free tonight. Want to get some dinner?"

"I've got a date with Jessica," Courtney replied. "We've been planning a girls' night to talk about the conference. Mostly I think she wants to tell me about a guy she met in New Orleans. They've been chatting each evening. She may be a little in love."

"Well, the conference had even more benefits than I realized. I'll tell Dad. He'll be happy to hear the meeting was helpful in more ways than one. Have fun with Jessica. And have a good weekend."

Courtney was surprised at Greg's easy acceptance of her plans for the evening. And he didn't ask her out for Saturday or Sunday. Her dread that he was working on budget cuts intensified. Good thing she was on the hunt for a new position.

Seeing Jessica across the restaurant, Courtney smiled at the big wave she received. Jessica reminded her of herself ten years ago, before she'd been tackled by life. Losing her parents had been a blow, but she and Sherry had taken it together. Losing Drew, though, had been a punch she'd weathered alone. It was hard to openly grieve the loss of a man with a sister planning her wedding. It wasn't fair to Sherry.

In contrast to her, Jessica's love of life oozed through her pores. Maybe Courtney would get some of that fire back. She was ready to try.

"Hey, Court, welcome to the weekend. I've ordered shrimp cocktail and artichoke dip. Unless you're allergic to seafood, like a certain ex of our boss's, that is. Was that a funny story, or what?"

"It was, Jessica. Greg was humble enough to tell it, though."

"Yeah, he's been different lately. Maybe because of you. What do you think?"

Courtney had a lot of thoughts she wasn't ready to reveal. "Maybe. We'll see. But you're on the witness stand tonight, not me. I'm ready to hear all about the guy from the Big Easy. I need details, girl!"

Jessica gave a lengthy account of her conversations with the man she'd met at the conference. Mac was a nurse in Panama City Beach, not too far from Destin, working at a hospital there. Per Jessica, he was the perfect man for her. Single, smart, gainfully employed, and nearby.

"Well then, why haven't you met him yet?" Courtney asked, eyes wide. "What's holding you two up?"

"It's happening next weekend," Jessica said. "I'll admit it, I'm scared. What if he's not as great as he seems? I'm tired of being disappointed."

"I understand completely. But we have to stay in the game, I guess. And we have to trust God through it all." Courtney sighed. "I wish it were as easy as I'm making it sound. 'Be still and know that I am God' used to be my favorite verse. But how do we 'be still' while also taking risks?"

Jessica sipped her water and shook her head. "I'm not a theologian by any stretch of the imagination, but I interpret that verse a little differently. I add a comma. 'Be still and know COMMA that I am God.' See the difference? We have to be quiet as God reveals Himself. We should accept his wisdom or knowing. *Not* be still and do nothing."

After a long pause, Courtney spoke. "Jessica, you are one wise woman. Just when I was thinking you were a carefree twenty-something, you blew me away. I love that interpretation." Courtney knew she was ready to give the relationship with Greg a real try. But she also knew she had to get away from the clinic he headed. Their relationship deserved a fighting chance. Her being at the clinic would only muddle their feelings.

After their food arrived, Courtney continued, "What are you doing next weekend with Mac? Do you want any girlfriend backup? I'd be glad to run interference if you need a phony call to bail out."

"You're the best, Court. We're meeting at a restaurant on Miramar Beach. It will be okay. But you live around there, so if needed I'll give you a call from the ladies' room and we can 'accidentally' run into each other. Just in case I need to be rescued."

"There's that word, rescued," Courtney mused. "It's been on my mind a lot lately. I think I was using Drew to rescue me, in a way. I have friends who were involved with men who had the means to help them through difficult times. Not that they chose men for that purpose. My friends had true love matches. Drew was my escape hatch. If I got tired of working at the college, or if the college closed my department, he could finance my next endeavor. Maybe he sensed that in me."

"Really?" Jessica almost gagged on her chip loaded with decadent dip. "You hardly strike me as a woman in need of rescue. My *sense* is that you're talking about the clinic. You're afraid you're going to be downsized, right? And be honest, because I sure am. For now, I'm going to stick and stay." Loading another corn chip with artichoke goodness, she paused for a loud crunch and continued, "Dr. McClure is a good guy, and one I think you should jump on asap, but he's gotta do what he's gotta do. You and I are the ones most likely not to succeed." Her somber assessment was accompanied by the usual Jessica grin.

"You read my mind, Jessica. If you're right, you'll be okay. You've got a roommate and a family to help you out. I, on the other hand, have a mortgage and a sister who's funding her big wedding." Courtney felt relieved to be talking openly about her fears. "Please keep this to yourself, but I'm looking around for a job with a little more security."

"You bet, Court. I'm as discreet as they come. No one will hear anything from me."

Courtney hoped Jessica was right. She wanted to be the one to tell Greg when she got another job. Not the office grapevine.

Ignoring his microwaved dinner, Greg looked at the financials for what seemed like the millionth time since his accountant had dropped them off at the office. Despite his best efforts with the new scheduling program and the improved insurance filings, the clinic was bleeding money. His CPA insisted it was temporary but admitted some short-term action wouldn't be a bad idea. "Short-term action" was code for layoffs or salary reductions. And when he studied the staff roster, it made the most managerial sense to start with payroll reductions for the newest employees. The ones his dad had hired. The ones he was bonding with more each day. Courtney and Jessica.

At worst, he was looking at a twenty percent cut in pay for the two newbies. He thought Jessica lived with a roommate, so she would be fine, he hoped. Courtney, however, had just purchased a beach condo and lived alone. Twenty percent would be a big hit for her. What would she do? Leave for a new job? Take in a renter? Maybe she wasn't stretched all that thin, and it wouldn't be a big deal for her. Maybe her deceased parents had left her well-fixed.

He knew he was dreaming. Twenty percent was real money, even if the cut were temporary. Just as he and Courtney were getting closer, he'd have to put this wrench in her life. He wondered what her elderly neighbor would advise her to do. Perhaps it was a good thing he was spending tomorrow with his father. Eric had been through this sort of mess and more when he'd been in charge of the clinic.

Saturday was the perfect day in gulf coast Florida. The morning sun promised some heat later, but with little of the humidity the later summer would bring. Greg balanced the decaf coffees he'd picked up, along with the egg-white sandwiches he'd added to his order. While Eric's cardiac problems weren't related to high cholesterol, it wouldn't hurt for each of them to watch their diets.

Eric's greeting boomed across the driveway. His dad sounded and looked good. Greg thanked God for his grace, and for the fact Eric's problem could be dealt with fairly simply.

After food and coffees, Eric looked at his son closely. "What's going on, Greg? You're concerned, and not about me. Is Taryn in the picture again?"

Eric's tension revealed his dread that Greg would confirm his fear. Barking a skeptical laugh at his protective father, Greg defused the atmosphere. "No, Dad, nothing like that. I'm pretty sure Taryn has found a more compliant guy than I could ever be. It's about the clinic."

"Things running tight? That's got to be it. You've got good staffing and a robust patient base, so those things don't merit a lot of worry. Fill me in."

Doing just that, Greg spent the better part of an hour informing his father about the dismal state of the clinic balance sheets. He concluded with his plan to reduce the salaries of the two newest hires. He was open about the cost of doing this both to Courtney and Jessica, and to himself.

"I'm in deep with Courtney, Dad. And now I have to cut her income for the immediate future, at least. But I see no other way out."

Eric looked stricken. "I'm sorry. I hired Courtney with an arrogant belief that I knew what was best for the clinic. And she's been doing excellent work, based on what you've told me. But twenty percent is a big cut. You know she'll be looking around, don't you?"

"If she's as smart as we both think she is, she's got feelers out already," Greg said. "In a way it could make things less complicated between us, but maybe not." He looked at his father. "She's going to think I betrayed her, Dad. How do I get around that?"

"I can help, Greg. I can be there when you talk to Courtney and Jessica, since I hired them both. Your decision will be framed as being in the best interest of the clinic. And I'll make it abundantly clear that both of them are top-notch employees, valued by both of us."

Greg appreciated his father's attempt. "Dad, you know that's not going to work. I'm leading the clinic now, and I'll tell them. But thanks. It means a lot."

Determined to use the chance to talk at a deeper level with his dad, Greg went on. "I've been thinking lately about the past, Dad. I'm sorry about our disputes, especially in regard to the clinic. Sometimes I figure my grief over Mom has been the reason, but I can't use it as an excuse." He stood and paced to the gas fireplace in his father's home. "My goal, my purpose, has too often been to outdo your work in diabetes medicine. Pretty shallow, isn't it? Anyway, I'm proud to be your son. I wanted to tell you that." Greg swallowed, hard.

Eric was tearing up as well. After a gulp of his own, he stood and hugged Greg. "Son, there's no need for all this." Stepping away and walking slowly back to the sofa, he said, "Maybe there is, though. Your words make it easier for me to admit some of my own shallowness and pride. One of my selfish concerns has been that you'll overshadow your old man, and that what I did for forty-five years won't matter much. Pitiful, right? I've realized lately that whatever you accomplish will be *your* achievement and mine to enjoy vicariously. God has been convicting me about this lately. I've been doing a lot of internal work, as a certain psychologist would say."

Both men laughed, and Eric clasped his hands. "More to the point, whatever you need to do for the sake of the clinic, and by extension for the sake of its patients, I give my full approval to. I'm sure Jackie has told you we had lean times in the past. But my decisions were always based on what was best for our patients. Each time I realized that our specialized clinic provided a service patients with diabetes couldn't get elsewhere. The bottom line is to do what seems right, Greg. You have my blessing."

After her Saturday chores and long walk on the beach, Courtney was settling in with the latest chick-lit novel when her phone rang. The number was unfamiliar, but knowing hospital paging systems often had unidentified numbers, she answered.

"Is this Dr. Courtney Bledsoe?" the voice asked.

"Speaking. Who's calling?"

"I apologize for phoning like this, but it's important. My name is Donna Pratt. I'm Minnie's daughter."

Courtney realized the area code was indeed from Indiana, so the woman's statement made sense. Then she got scared and blurted, "Is Minnie okay? We just talked last night. She was tired, but she wasn't coughing much."

"Mom is fine," Donna said. "Well, she's not really fine, which is why I'm calling. Mom has told me and my sister Candi what a good friend you've been to her. She also wanted me to tell you about her illness." Donna stopped, stifling a sob. "We've all made the decision to engage hospice for Mom's end-stage COPD. She's in agreement but wanted me to ask you a huge favor. We'd pay you of course."

Confused, Courtney replied. "Donna, I'm not a medical doctor. Or a medical professional of any sort, except for psychology. The hospice staff will care for Minnie."

"We know all that, but Mom wanted to ask if we could pay you an hourly rate to stay overnight with her. Hospice comes a couple of times a day, but family or other paid caregivers are expected to be there at night. Candi and I have families to tend to in Indiana. We'll be there when hospice says to come, but in the meantime, you seemed like the perfect solution."

"I'm honored," Courtney said without thinking of all she was committing to. "I'd like to talk to Minnie before I agree, though."

"Certainly," Donna said. "Thanks for considering it, Dr. Bledsoe. Mom has spoken often about you and how much she values your friendship."

After the usual closing pleasantries, Courtney ended the call and stared at the ocean outside her balcony. As always, the sound of the waves calmed her. She would do it. She would be with Minnie during the woman's last days. She was signing up for lots of pain, but in a way, it made some perverse sense. Her parents had been alone when they died, but Minnie wouldn't be. God willing, her daughters would make it to Destin in time, but if not, Courtney would be there.

The next few weeks were a blur. Greg told Courtney and Jessica about the need for reductions in their salaries. He was surprised by their understanding. As expected, Jessica said she could weather the lean times because she had a roommate and kept her spending low. She emphasized her point by saying, "I'm as tight as a tick, Dr. McClure."

After Jessica left the room, Courtney was open about her search for another job, but sweet in her response to Greg's bad news. "It's truly going to be all right, Greg. The clinic will come back stronger than ever. And as I've thought in the past, we can be whatever we're meant to be, without all the layers of a shared workplace."

"What will you do?" Greg asked, feeling both relief and sadness. "I'll miss you around here."

"I'm going to be working for Cindy Patterson," Courtney said, smiling at the thought. "The job is part eating disorders and part psychoeducation at local colleges. I may move into working at the hospital mood disorders center after the psychoed piece is done. I'll be all right, and so will you," she repeated.

"What will you do about the psychologist position? Have you thought about a contracted position, sort of an as-needed job?"

"That's probably what we'll do for now. Who knows? You may end up treating some of our patients at the mood disorders center. Full circle, huh?"

They hugged, and despite his desire, Greg didn't ask Courtney to dinner that evening. She'd just given her notice; the timing was off. Very off.

Courtney went back to her office and to the clients she had waiting. Shutting his door, Greg finished his paperwork and spent the rest of the afternoon staring at the walls. He needed a plan, not for the clinic but for Courtney. He wasn't about to lose this woman. Once she was working elsewhere, he'd need to ensure they connected often. Daily, if he had his way.

After her final two weeks at the clinic ended, Courtney relished having a couple of weeks of vacation. It was unpaid vacation, unfortunately, but the free time was welcome. Saying goodbye to her patients had been more draining than expected, with the exception of Mandy Eller.

"You mean I'll still get to see you at the IOP? That's terrific!" Mandy enthused. Looking slyly at her mother, she continued. "I'll keep you posted about Dr. McClure. And I'll let him know what's up with you." Everyone laughed, though Courtney thought she'd welcome the intel from Mandy. Despite the girl's difficulties, she was obviously a shrewd judge of relationships.

On her first evening away from the clinic, Courtney packed her overnight bag and went to Minnie's apartment. When she'd learned that Courtney had agreed to be her "night-sitter", Minnie had ordered new bunk bed mattresses. Despite Courtney's protests, Minnie had insisted.

Between coughs, she had announced, "Anyone kind enough to stay with me until the Lord calls me home deserves a decent bed." Minnie was now on full-time oxygen, which helped some, but Courtney knew the reprieve would be short-lived. Hospice was there for a reason.

After several games of gin rummy, Minnie was too keyed up to go to bed. "I think we need to talk, Dr. Courtney. My girls told me you'd quit your job, which wasn't all that surprising. But give me the background. Surely Dr. McClure wasn't too touchy-feely. Or was he?" she asked, arching her brow.

"No, nothing like that," Courtney answered. "He had to reduce expenses, and the two newest employees had to take a salary cut. *This* new employee's budget didn't like the sound of that. My next post will be full of variety, part-time at the eating disorders clinic and the rest with outreach and the depression clinic."

"And this will give both of you doctors time to get to know each other better. I think God's looking out for you, Courtney. All this gives me more motivation to fight my illness. I want to see how things turn out!"

As do I, Courtney thought, as she tucked Minnie under her heavy covers.

Settling in on her bunk, her new pager jingled. She wasn't an official employee of the hospital yet, but she'd been given her ID badge and a pager when she filled out forms at HR. She called the number on display hoping, as she had on her first day at the Diabetes Care Clinic, that it was a wrong number.

"Hey, Court, it's Greg. How are things going?"

"They're going about as expected at ten o'clock at night," she grumbled. "I'm in bed with a good book." No need to tell Greg she was sitting with Minnie; he'd probably offer to float her some cash, thinking she was destitute. "And how did you get this number?"

Chuckling with pride at his detective skills, he said, "I've got privileges at the hospital, remember? I just called the switchboard and asked for you."

"Well, since I can't help with your patients anymore, what do you need?" Courtney was annoyed but not sure why. Maybe she'd hoped for a breather from Greg McClure.

"I need a lot more time with you, that's one thing. The office is slowly adjusting to life without your presence, your balance, your kindness. And I'm trying to adjust, but not very well. When can we see each other again? Could you make dinner tomorrow night? I'll be in the clinic until seven, but I'd be up for an eight o'clock reservation."

Not wanting to talk about Minnie with her only a closed door away, Courtney hedged. "My evenings are booked after eight, Greg. Maybe brunch this weekend?"

"Brunch. Okay. I'll pick you up on Saturday at eleven. I'm missing you already, Courtney." His disappointment was clear. He paused, waiting for Courtney to explain further. Hearing nothing, he ended the call. "See you on Saturday. Looking forward to it."

Courtney stared at the bunk above her. Greg wanted to see her. He was deflated when she said her evenings were full. She would explain later. In the meantime, she had a weekend date to look forward to.

What would she and Greg talk about after he updated her on the clinic? She would tell him about Minnie, of course, but would there be silence after that? What did the two of them really have in common, other than an interest in the care of diabetic patients? Her decision to leave the clinic was now looking like a bad move. Would distance really make Greg's heart grow fonder? Was she now resorting to bad cliches to rationalize the end of her involvement with Greg?

Chapter Nine

After Courtney's dismissal, Greg stared at his phone. She had been clear about her desire to avoid him during the week. He tried to be positive; maybe it just meant she was busy with other projects before she went back to work full-time. He clung to that hope. Saturday brunch became his touchstone for the week.

Overall, things were going well at the clinic. Courtney had referred her clients to other practitioners in the area. Not an ideal solution, but they seemed to adjust quickly, telling Greg about their work with the new therapists. The staff was settling in, too. Jessica asked daily when her salary would be back to its full amount which he found amusing at first, then irritating. But what did he expect? Roommate or not, Jessica had to be feeling the pinch. By Saturday morning, his nerves were shredded.

Driving to Courtney's condo, he marveled at the grit it had taken for her to leave all that was familiar to come to Florida. Sure, her ex had been terrible, but she could have moved to another place in Indiana. Or to a midwestern location that was drivable to and from all that was familiar to her. But she'd chosen Destin, or more specifically, Miramar Beach. He recalled she'd mentioned intolerance to the cold weather, but again there were warmer places closer to Indiana. He'd have to ask, along with the dozens of other questions about Courtney crowding his mind.

As he pulled into the back entrance that housed the parking area, Greg noticed Courtney waiting for him. As always, she was gorgeous, dressed in snug-fitting slacks and a ruffled sleeveless top. But she looked a little tired, which was odd given that she was enjoying two weeks of downtime before she started her new job.

"Hi, Greg," Courtney said as she slipped into the passenger seat. "I thought I'd meet you here to make it easier to get to our brunch. I'm starved."

He leaned over, brushing her coppery hair out of her face. After a kiss he'd been hungering for, he answered, "I'm hungry, too, but mostly for the sight of you. How are you doing?"

"I'm good. I should be asking you that question also. But we'll talk at our meal." Courtney smiled at him. "I've been a little hungry for you, too." She turned away, almost embarrassed at her admission.

After they were seated at their beachside table, Greg took Courtney's hands in his. "Seriously, I've *missed* you. If I didn't care for you so much, I'd be hoping you've been miserable, too."

Courtney threw her head back and laughed; the laugh that made things right in Greg's world. He'd forgotten how much her pleasure eased his mind. When Courtney was happy, he almost believed things would be right again in his world. The clinic would be financially viable, his father would be healthy and whole, and he would be with a woman who could be a true life partner.

"You don't look miserable, Dr. Greg McClure. You look as good as ever. 'Hunky' is a word I always use to describe you, though I'm giving myself away. My sources tell me you've been a little irritable, however. Are you okay? And what about your dad? Is he going to be all right?"

"Dad is fine and sends his best. He was happy we were going to meet. He's always been one of your biggest fans."

The waiter took their orders and Greg marveled at Courtney's forgiving metabolism. His order of fruit and an egg white omelet contrasted with hers of Eggs Benedict with home fries. But then, she probably walked the beach at least daily.

After a sip of her mimosa, Courtney continued with her questions. "Thank the Good Lord Eric is on the mend. I've been praying for him. What about you, Greg? How is the clinic doing?"

"I'm fine, especially now that we're together. The clinic is doing better. My accountant says the insurance payments will catch up in a few months. Then I'm going to have to reinstate Jessica as a full-timer, though that will be with mixed feelings on my part." Greg's wink accompanied his statement.

"Yes, Jessica can be a little assertive, maybe at times aggressive," Courtney agreed. "But she's a fine dietitian, and she's been a great friend to me. She calls me every day after work to check in."

"And to report on me?" Greg asked. "My guess is she's your source describing me as irritable. In my defense, she pesters me several times a day about her part-time status. I have a perverse notion to keep her on eighty-percent salary for a while longer. The clinic is very peaceful on her day off."

Taking Courtney's hand again, Greg looked at her carefully. "Court, you look a little tired to me. Are you truly okay? Is there anything I can do to help? Dad wanted me to offer you a loan from his personal funds if you needed that kind of assistance."

Courtney huffed in response and looked torn as she formulated an answer. "I wasn't going to mention this, but I'm working as an overnight sitter for my neighbor. She's been put on hospice and sleeps well, but watching her decline pulls me apart some nights." Wiping away the tear escaping her right eye, she continued. "She's one of the most courageous women I've ever met. We've been doing a lot of life reminiscing; her memories almost always have an object lesson that applies to my life."

Greg was gentle as he asked about Minnie's illness, family, and Courtney's involvement in the woman's care. After he'd gotten the big picture, he couldn't help giving his two cents. "This must be awful for you, Courtney. The grief over Minnie has to bring back the loss of your parents. Are you sure this is the right thing for you to be doing?"

Pulling her hand away, Courtney shook her head. "She's my *friend*, Greg. Friends do what needs to be done, even if it's hard. Her daughters are wonderful. They've made arrangements to alternate their visits when my new job starts. If Minnie lasts that long."

Feeling Courtney's reference to friends *doing what should be done when things were hard* was directed at him, Greg was silenced. How could he convince this woman he'd done everything in his power to save her job? Why was she forgetting her statement that it would be beneficial for them to work at separate locations?

"Message received," he said, taking her hand again. "As your friend, and as someone who hopes to be a lot more, I respect your devotion to Minnie. She sounds like a wonderful person." He looked into Courtney's expressive eyes and took a risk. "Also, I need to remind you that you thought it could be beneficial to our relationship if we worked at different places. Is that still the case, or is your emphasis on true friendship a way to get rid of me?"

Grasping his hand tighter, Courtney replied, "No, I sure don't want to get rid of you, Greg. I want more than friendship, too. But I'm afraid of feeling too much for you. My heart doesn't mend easily. And I still think it's best we're working apart."

Breathing hard, as if she were seeking courage, she took another sip of her coffee. "Here's the thing. It seems as though I've always been linked to a man professionally. First it was a guy in my cohort in grad school. We were going to take jobs in the same city, blah, blah, blah. It didn't happen. He was all about Seattle, and I landed at GCC. Then Drew came to Gordon and before I knew it, I was his best referral source and girlfriend. And boom, I come to Destin and I'm kissing my boss!" She stared at the waves outside the restaurant. "I'm kind of a goof, huh? I just don't want to repeat that old pattern. You're too important to me for that to happen again. Hence, my need to find a new job when you reduced my salary."

"I see," Greg said, though he really didn't. He decided to let her keep talking.

"And Jessica's not the only frugal employee you had," she continued. "I lived in a tiny studio apartment above a garage in Gordon. I banked the bulk of my salary from GCC. I could have dealt with your twenty-percent cut, but it was a good way to exit and see what we really had between us. So, here I am being totally honest. What do you make of it?"

Greg smiled. The only thing that had registered from Courtney's speech was that he was too important to her to lose. "Let's eat before this delicious food gets cold. Thanks for your honesty. And you are *not* a goof, Courtney. You're the best woman I've ever met. I'm honored to have you in my life, even if you did quit working for me."

Courtney finally relaxed enough to enjoy her eggs. She was proud of herself for being open with Greg. In fact, he seemed pleased. Go figure. After brunch he suggested a drive around the coast, showing her the places she hadn't had time to explore, including Seaside and Panama City Beach.

"Wow, such beauty all around," she said. "Do you ever get tired of the perfect weather and mild winters? And the constant presence of the ocean? It's heaven to me."

"Almost heaven, I guess. The summers can be hot and humid, as you're about to discover. And though we don't get many hurricanes, when they come, they can be devastating. But I agree; I wouldn't want to live anywhere else." He paused. "What about you?"

Knowing his question was a loaded one, Courtney decided to tease. "For now, this is great. But who knows what the future will bring?"

Greg chuckled, realizing her game. He pulled into her condo drive.

"Why don't you come up for coffee?" Courtney asked. It was time to invite him to her home, she thought. She had taken the risk to be honest, and now she had to risk being up close and personal in a private environment.

"I'd love that," Greg said, as he parked in the attached parking garage. "I'd really love it."

Once upstairs after the elevator ride, Courtney gave Greg the nickel tour of her limited space. "Here are my luxury bunk beds," she said. "My bedroom is actually the guest room when friends and family visit. I sleep on the lower bunk. My kitchen is small, but efficient. I've baked countless breads and pastries here. And here's the crowning glory of my place." Opening the sliding glass doors, they stepped into her beachfront concrete balcony, which Courtney had furnished with second-hand wicker pieces. "There's no better place for coffee while I watch the sun come up. I feel close to God and all His strength when I start each day."

"This view is glorious. Your apartment is reflective of you, too. I recognize the bold colors and comfortable atmosphere from your decor at the office. Remember how I joked that you'd broken the budget with those slipcovers?"

Leaning in, he took her in his arms. Courtney's mind was a jumble. She wanted his kiss, badly. But she also wanted to be sure, to be safe. As wise Minnie said just last night, she had to take a risk if she was ever going to hit the jackpot. Evidently Minnie and her husband had done some gambling on their cruises; many of her tidbits were laced with "going for the big payoff" metaphors.

After a lingering kiss, Courtney led Greg back inside. "I hate to do this, but I promised Minnie I'd bake her cinnamon rolls for tomorrow's breakfast. Would you mind if I worked in spurts while you watch whatever sports event you can find on the television?"

Greg shrugged and began to work the remote. Finding a European soccer game, he asked, "Couldn't you do that this evening? You're putting me at arms' length, Court."

His forlorn look made Courtney smile. "I'll be with you in a few minutes. The dough has to rise a couple of times, so I can't put this off until tonight."

Back on the sofa with Greg, she leaned her head against his chest. "This feels so right. I have a sort of peace with you that I've not had with other men. In grad school there was a subtle competition with my boyfriend. And with Drew the business always came first; my referrals were dissected like bugs under a microscope. I love...being with you without any other agenda pulling us apart."

Greg looked at her carefully. "I was hoping you'd say you loved me," he said. "But I'll take what you can give for now." He hugged her tighter and focused on soccer.

Nestling in Greg's arms, Courtney drifted off. Awakening with a start, she wiped a little drool off her cheek. "How long was I out?" she asked.

Kissing her head, Greg squeezed her closer. "About thirty minutes," he said. "Really, Courtney, I'm worried about the overnight commitment you've made. Are you sure it's not going to be a burden?"

"Well, I am being paid a little," she said. "But you're right – it's a burden of sorts. Isn't that the point of it all, though? That we'll be lucky enough to have people in our lives willing to take our burdens from us?"

"I guess so. But my goal is that someday you'll let me be one of those who can help with your burdens."

Courtney cupped Greg's face in her hands while she studied his troubled expression. "Maybe I will, someday. For now, I really like having you as my baking buddy." The kitchen timer went off, and she scurried to get back to the rolls.

After the cinnamon rolls were baked and cooled, and after Greg was allowed to sample one, he and Courtney enjoyed the chance to just be together. There was no pressure, other than that of enjoying a fresh-baked treat. At six o'clock, she reminded him of her night job.

"I hate to make you leave, but I've got to shower and get ready for Minnie duty," she said. "I pack a book, my Bible, snacks, and a deck of cards. Sometimes she can't sleep, and it helps her to stay up and beat me at gin rummy."

Driving home, Greg wondered about the Indiana woman who fascinated him so. She was letting him in, but slowly. Her allure was potent. It was all he could do to refrain from suggesting he join her in the shower. Kissing her, holding her, sniffing the scent of whatever perfume she had chosen that day – it all reminded him of why he'd been so unhappy with Taryn. Unlike Taryn, Courtney didn't have a signature scent. She wore whatever suited her mood. Courtney hadn't even bothered with makeup today, but she looked beautiful with her sun-kissed cheeks and red hair glistening in the light. Taryn, on the other hand, was always perfectly attired, made up, and ready for controlling the seduction she inevitably had planned for him. In contrast, Courtney was gentle, sweet, and honest. No fake emotions from her; he'd seen her temper at the office, and today he'd seen her sadness at her friend Minnie's decline. And she sure didn't want to seduce or be seduced. Love was too important to her.

Did he love her? He'd hoped she would say she loved him, but she'd caught herself in time. Had he loved Taryn? He'd had plenty of fun with her, but that wasn't love. She wasn't wife material.

Wife material? He wasn't ready for a wife. He could barely pay his own meager salary out of the clinic's earnings. More to the point, he doubted he was ready to pay the emotional price of being a good husband, as his reference to "wife material" indicated. What kind of man put women into such categories? The kind who had only pleasure and gain on his mind. Greg used to be that guy, but now he didn't know where he fit.

As he mused his life situation, his phone rang. "What's up, Dad? Are you okay? Is the pacemaker working as it should?"

Eric chuckled. "My, you're turning into quite the mother hen," he said. "Just like your mom, God rest her. I'm fine, but something told me you might not be. Want to talk?"

Greg settled into his leather chair as he put the latest soccer match on mute. "Yes, Dad, I need to talk. How did you know?"

"I remembered you had a brunch date. It's now late in the evening, and you're home. That could be a bad sign. How was your day with Courtney?"

"It was good," Greg hedged, sinking further into his seat. "She's been sitting overnight with a terminally ill neighbor, which explains our lack of evening activities."

He stared at his television and tried to explain his confusion to his father. "But we had a good talk. She opened up to me, Dad, about her past and her fear of being involved. Not sure how I'm going to get past that."

"But you want to, right? You're answering my other question, Greg. I was going to ask if you still had feelings for her. You obviously do."

"Yes, I do. But I'm miserable. Things were easy with Taryn. We each knew the other's agenda. She wanted to trap me into marriage, and I wanted to have fun. I'm not proud of that, but the rules were clear. With Courtney, I feel like I'm sinking into an abyss. If I let her in, I'm in it for the long haul. There's no halfway point with her."

"Sounds like she's not the only one afraid of being involved," Eric said. Greg could envision his father's smirk across the connection.

"All I can do is share my experience," Eric continued. "I'd been with several women before your mom. They were good people, as is Taryn, though she'd be a disaster for you if you ever married. Anyway, when I met your mother, I was ready for another fling."

"Go on, Dad." Greg was surprised. He'd thought his parents had known they were meant to be together from day one. So much for his assumptions.

"Well, your mother made it clear she was in no mood for a player. She wanted the real deal and was willing to shut me down when she figured me out. Took me quite a while to convince her I was serious about her."

"What changed? Why didn't you move on?" Greg asked.

"Same thing that's got you so confused. I realized I finally had the courage for a real, committed relationship. I was ready to be with a woman who deserved all of me. Scary, huh?"

"Frightening," Greg mumbled. "But accurate. Thanks for talking to me, Dad. Have I ever told you that you're brilliant?"

Father and son laughed together and ended the call. Greg felt better and sent Courtney a text message, hoping she'd have a peaceful night with Minnie. He closed the message with a heart emoji. He was a goner. He loved Courtney and he was going to have to find the guts to tell her. Soon.

Chapter Ten

Just as Courtney was ready to turn off the light attached to Minnie's lower bunk, her phone jingled. Who could be calling this late on a Saturday night? She answered and heard a tense Cindy Patterson breathe a sigh of relief.

"Thanks for picking up, Courtney. I know it's too late to be calling, but I'm researching all my options. Our IOP therapist is going to be out this week due to a death in the family. I've got the Wednesday and Thursday sessions covered, but Monday, as in the day after tomorrow, is open. I know you're not an employee yet, but is there any way you could cover from four to seven on Monday? The format is the usual: you do a psychoeducational piece at the start to get the patients talking, then you break for a snack, and finally you process what's been going on in their lives, how it was to eat a 'forbidden' food, and so on. By the way, the snack for Monday is a two-hundred calorie, chocolate-covered ice cream bar, so I've given you fair warning."

Courtney laughed at her new boss's turmoil.

Cindy was usually the epitome of cool. "I'd be glad to help out. My human resources paperwork is completed, so that's no issue. I guess I'm a real employee. What topic do I need to prepare in the next thirty-six hours?"

"You have free rein," Cindy said. "Do you have anything from your job in Indiana? Surely you did presentations at GCC."

"I've got several that might work," Courtney answered. "There's one on the trap of comparing yourself with others that always generated a lot of discussion. Would that work with your patients?"

"Perfect!" Cindy yelled, again betraying the stress she was under. "The current group is aged from tween to mid-teens, with one older patient who may be starting IOP this week. That topic is huge with them, especially with their constant focus on social media. They're always sure that others have the perfect life, body, family, and on and on. I'll meet you at the center a little before four on Monday. Do we have a deal?"

"We do. See you then." Courtney settled in under the covers, noting there was no sound or movement in Minnie's room. Her friend was sleeping well, at least for now. And if Courtney was going to work on Monday until seven, then dash back to tend to Minnie, she needed to get some sleep herself.

Sunday and Monday were spent walking the beach, doing shopping and household chores, and baking sugar cookies for Minnie. She called Minnie and her daughters about the late start to her sitting on Monday and got the clearance that there was no problem. Now she just had to face a group of hostile young women and convince them to honor their souls and bodies by not caring what others said or looked like. As if. But she would give it her all.

Cindy Patterson welcomed Courtney as she walked into the eating disorders office. "Thanks again for filling in," she said. "All the therapists, including yours truly, are booked solid today, and one of us had a client who needed hospitalization. It's been quite a Monday."

"What about backup if I need help?" Courtney asked, panicked at the thought of being in the center by herself for three hours. "If there's a crisis, what's the procedure?"

"You won't be alone. I and two other therapists will be in our offices with our patients. We're just down the south hall. If you need any help, just knock on our doors."

Cindy showed Courtney the IOP room and the snack area. As Courtney grounded herself to the new surroundings, patients began to arrive.

"Dr. Bledsoe, what are you doing here?" the familiar voice called. "I thought you didn't start until next week."

"I'm filling in today, Mandy," Courtney said. "How are things with you?"

Suitable small talk took a few minutes, and by the time everyone was settled and introduced, Courtney began her presentation. The dangers of comparison were highlighted, and as Courtney had hoped, the participants talked without reservation. The session flew by, and soon it was time for a snack.

"What's the snack today?" Mandy asked. "It's supposed to be a forbidden food, and I've had nightmares about the possibilities."

This led to more fervent discussion about the whole mistaken notion of forbidden foods, which was not as well received as education about the comparison trap. Eventually, though, each girl had eaten her ice cream bar. A few looked agonized, so Courtney had each practice a round of relaxation breathing.

"Now we get to talk about whatever we want," Mandy told her. "Usually, we go around the room and each girl can discuss her current troubles."

Nodding her understanding, Courtney took her own breath and asked, "Who wants to begin?"

After the requisite pause and shared glances, the girl opposite Mandy spoke. "I want to get into the comparison thing more," she said. "My social feeds are full of perfect girls, I swear. How am I supposed to feel? And how am I supposed to not compare myself with them? It's impossible."

Fighting her urge to hug the girl and tell her about God's love, Courtney looked around the room. Good group therapy would come more from peers than from her. Thanking God when others chimed in to challenge the young girl's hopelessness, Courtney handled the rest of the session.

As the patients were leaving, Mandy lingered behind. "So really, Dr. B, how are you?" she asked with intense seriousness. "Do you miss the Diabetes Care Clinic?"

"I'm fine, Mandy. I miss my buddies, but I connect with them often. More importantly, I'm glad to see you working hard on your therapy here. You're a smart young woman and a good friend to the other girls."

Ignoring Courtney's attempt to divert the focus, Mandy smiled. "I'm doing well. But you should know something, Dr. B. Dr. McClure is looking lonely. Very. Very. Lonely. Maybe you should give him a call."

Smiling as she remembered Mandy's blatant attempt at matchmaking, Courtney entered her apartment. After making sure things were in order, she hustled to Minnie's condo and let herself in. Minnie called out, obviously glad to have company.

"My goodness, I'm sure glad to see you," she said. "I'm fine, but just a little lonely. How did your group therapy go?"

"Very well, thanks," Courtney said as she arranged her bunk. "Do you want to talk a while? I can make some tea."

"Lovely," Minnie said. "I enjoy tea at this time of night. Not quite bedtime, but still quiet and already dark. Sort of that in-between time, when the world is peaceful but not yet in slumber."

Courtney looked at her neighbor, who was never this philosophical. "What's going on, Minnie? Anything bothering you?"

Minnie smiled. "You saw through me, Courtney. That's why you're a good therapist. I've just been thinking about life and of course, death. I know how things stand, what with hospice here every day and my cough never letting up. I'll be meeting the Lord soon."

After a deep cough that offered no relief, Minnie continued, "I was thinking about when I let my gray hair grow out, of all things." Noting Courtney's puzzled look, she added, "Took me long enough. I think I was almost seventy and still coloring my hair. That's okay for some women, but what a hassle! So, when it finally came into its natural color, I liked it! It was mostly white, but had just enough salt-and-pepper streaking to look chic, or so I thought. Anyway, at seventy, I was finally comfortable enough to be my true self, at least in terms of my hair. Dumb, huh?"

"Not dumb, but maybe a reflection of our culture and of our need to feel young."

"As my hubby always said, 'There's an easy way to do things and a hard way to do things.' He thought the key to getting along in this world was to figure out the easy way without losing yourself in the process. Who knew that not having to schedule hair appointments would free me up so much? It was a real turning point."

Courtney was now truly confused. "I don't get it, Minnie. I'm sure you were always your true self, as you say."

Minnie focused her steely eyes on Courtney. "No, I'd been denying what was real. I was seventy, not fifty-something. I tell you it was liberating. And you could learn from this, girl."

Laughing, Courtney challenged the older woman. "Believe it or not, I don't color my hair. If I did, it wouldn't be this crazy red. I'd be a blonde, or a ravishing brunette."

Now they both laughed. Minnie tried to explain, "What I meant was, you can take an easier road with Dr. McClure than you realize. Enjoy your new job, see if you like it, and let him fight his own financial battles at the clinic. Live your own life without looking over your shoulder to see how he's doing.

He's a grown man and you're a grown woman. Have a relationship without all the messiness of a shared job. Doesn't that make sense?"

"I guess," Courtney admitted. "A mutual patient made a point of telling me this evening that Dr. McClure looked very lonely. You're saying I should focus on him, but not on his work? That doesn't seem right; the clinic is a big part of his identity."

"Sure, it is. But not his whole identity. And based on what you've shared with me, it would do him good to see that. He needs to have some separation from work, from his father's past success, even from his own competitive ambition."

Coughing to the point of almost gagging, Minnie adjusted her oxygen. "I need to get some sleep, Courtney. But I'm just saying you and Greg are both strong personalities. He could consume yours if you let him. If you don't, that is, if you can be yourself separate from him, it could be magic. The magic could be effortless, easy. Understand?"

Shaking her head, Courtney helped Minnie get settled under her covers. Unpacking Minnie's words of wisdom would take more energy than she had this evening. Halfway out of the room, Courtney turned and went back to place a gentle kiss on Minnie's cheek.

Greg looked at the calendar, astonished that Courtney had only been gone a few weeks. The contract psychologist, a male per his specific (and probably illegal) instructions to the hiring agency, was doing a good job. Patients seemed to like him well enough, and he didn't contradict Greg's input nearly as often as Courtney had. So why was he missing her so much? Granted, they'd had some weekend meals and a few walks on the beach. But in terms of a real dating relationship, their time together felt distanced and somewhat formal. Maybe that old lady she was sitting for had schooled Courtney on Victorian courtship guidelines.

It seemed simple to him. He had to get Courtney back on full-time staff at the clinic. The balance sheets looked promising. She could come back soon and there would be no more problems with justifying her salary. Even Jessica was back to working five days per week. He'd talk to Courtney about her return this weekend at brunch.

Brunch! What he wouldn't give for an evening together. An evening under the stars with the ocean waves hitting the shore next to the most expensive restaurant he could find in the Florida panhandle. A real date, for which Courtney would wear that sexy dress she'd displayed in New Orleans. That felt so long ago, a lifetime.

Brought back to reality by the light on his phone, Greg realized his next patient was waiting. Mandy and her mom greeted him in the exam room opposite his office.

"Hey, Dr. McClure!" Mandy sang as he entered. Cathy rolled her eyes but seemed relaxed and positive.

"Hi, Miss Eller," Greg said. "How have you been doing? Should I trust the great lab values and your glowing skin? Or are you hiding yet another secret about how you've decided to beat diabetes?"

"Ha. Very funny," Mandy said. "You can trust my labs. I still think I'm too fat, but the eating disorders group has been great. I don't feel so alone when I beat up on myself. And there's even a new woman with diabetes who fought anorexia. She's pregnant, after she and her husband had given up on having kids! She's shared a lot with the group. Actually, she sounds just like I used to sound."

"I think Mandy's trying to say she's more hopeful," Cathy said. "Meeting other girls, and now a young woman with the same challenges has brought her a lot of peace. I can't thank you enough for referring her to the eating disorders clinic."

Feeling guilty and therefore forced into honesty, Greg replied, "It was Dr. Bledsoe's idea. To be fair, she had to convince me. But I'm really glad to hear you're doing better, Mandy. You have a full life ahead of you. Just remember that when you get discouraged."

"I won't forget," Mandy said with a knowing smile. "But what about Dr. Bledsoe? I saw her at the IOP session a while ago and she looked sad; really sad. I think she misses working here." Mandy took a dramatic pause, gazing at Greg's institutional art-work. "Maybe she misses you, though. That would make sense, don't you think?"

"Well, young lady, I'm not sure that's suitable talk for a diabetes checkup. Thanks for your concern, though."

Mandy harrumphed and the exam finished quickly. As Mandy made her way to the outer office, Greg looked at Cathy. "I'm thrilled with Mandy's progress. But how about you? You're still grieving your husband. Is there anything the clinic can do to help you?"

Startled by Greg's concern, Cathy blushed. "No, Dr. McClure. Thanks for your offer. Actually, I'm in counseling with my pastor. He's been a great help and referred me to a support group. He even suggested Mandy get treatment at the eating disorders center right before you did. He's a good therapist."

Watching Cathy walk down the hall, Greg was annoyed. At himself. Even the pastor at the Ellers' church had seen the need for Mandy to get treatment for her eating disorder. Instead, he'd missed the boat on that, probably because he had been engaged in the power struggle with Courtney. Instead of welcoming her to his clinic, he'd been intent on showing his superiority. Now she was working for the hospital, sitting overnight with a terminally ill friend and avoiding him like the plague.

He had to get Courtney back on his staff. The next time they were together, probably for a chaste brunch and a round of baking for Minnie, he'd tell her. The clinic needed her and so did he.

Courtney smiled at Greg's latest text. He was turning on the charm, determined to have a "proper date" this weekend. According to Greg, that meant she had to ask for an evening off from Minnie's care. Little did he know Minnie's younger daughter was in town for a week. Courtney had plenty of evenings free.

Deciding to call rather than endure a lengthy round of cryptic text messages, she was surprised when he answered on the first ring.

"Courtney, it's great to hear from you," Greg said, his smile coming across the connection. "It seems like forever. So, can you get away for a dinner date this weekend? Or are we stuck with brunch? I'm not sure how much more overpriced breakfast food I can stand."

"Poor thing," Courtney teased. "As it happens, for the next week I have my evenings to myself. Minnie's younger daughter is staying with her. It's done her a world of good."

"How about tonight?" Greg asked, impatience and aggravation coloring his question. "And tomorrow night? And every night until the daughter leaves?"

"Hold on, mister. I've got other things to do, as do you. Tomorrow night would work. Tonight, I've got a presentation to tweak. My GCC slides are a little stale for current IOP presentations."

Jumping in before she could change her mind, Greg issued orders, "Great. I'll pick you up in your condo drive at six o'clock tomorrow. Dress fancy. Maybe that blue clingy thing you wore in New Orleans."

"Yessir," Courtney said as she saluted the phone. "Are you mad at me, Greg? You seem a little stressed."

"I'm not mad. Just missing you and a little perturbed you didn't let me know you weren't working evenings."

Courtney debated what to say next. She'd planned to call Greg midweek, after she got her thoughts about him in some sort of order. No such luck; he confused her as much as ever.

"I'm sorry," she said. "I just needed some time, for some things." Laughing at herself, she added, "Did that clear things up?"

"Not a bit, but I'm glad to hear you laugh. See you tomorrow."

As promised, Greg picked her up at six. Complying with his demand, she wore the blue dress from New Orleans. Smiling at the jabs she'd received about her inappropriate choice for a friend's wedding, she entered Greg's car.

"You didn't give me a chance to get your door," he grumbled. "I'm trying to make tonight special. And what's so funny?"

"Not funny. Sweet. I was thinking about our time in New Orleans."

"Not so sweet, either. I recall some significant body heat in the hallway as we got to your room. It was mighty pleasant, but not sweet."

Courtney smiled at Greg. He was different tonight. More focused on her. Intent on making the night special. Drew popped into her thoughts. He'd never been like this. His focus had always been singularly on himself. If nothing else came of her relationship with Greg, at least she had this memory of what it was like when a man was totally into her.

"Thanks for wearing the dress," Greg said. "As always, you look great." Helping her out of the car when they arrived at the ocean-side restaurant, his arm circled her waist. "But the dress is a little loose. Are you working too much? Losing weight?"

Courtney sighed. Unsure if she appreciated his concern or resented his assessment, she looked at the dark circles under his eyes.

"And you, my doctor friend, look a little tired. Are you sleeping?"

"Touché," Greg said. "I didn't mean to smother you. Yes, I'm tired. Tired of missing you."

They were taken to their table, which offered a perfect view of the incoming tide. After drinks and appetizers were ordered, Greg spoke again.

"Let me start by saying how happy I am to see you. I wasn't kidding about missing you. Our contract psychologist is a good guy, but he doesn't argue with me nearly enough. Want to come back?"

Courtney flashed a smile, hoping to defuse Greg's serious request. He'd tried to hide behind his joke, but it was obvious he wanted her back at the clinic. "Greg, it's wonderful to be missed. But it's also wonderful to be at a job I love, with independence and variety. I'm all over the Destin area giving my presentations and just when I get tired of that, I land at the eating disorders center or mood and anxiety clinic for the rest of the week. It suits me well." Leaning over the small table, she stroked his face. "That said, I miss you, too. But I believe we're better working apart and being a couple after hours. What about you?"

Mumbling something she couldn't decipher, Greg cleared his throat. "No, I disagree. I want to be near you all the time. We were doing well until I had to cut hours. Is that what this is about? I promise that will never happen again."

Bristling, Courtney withdrew her hand. "Greg, you're not hearing me. I love what I'm doing now. And I may even love you, but it's better for us to work apart. As Minnie says, 'There's an easy way to do things and a hard way.' I think our easy way is to have our professional lives separate from our personal lives."

"Minnie? You're taking advice from an eighty-something woman?"

"What about you? I'm sure you've talked to your father about us. What's he have to say?"

Greg looked stern but couldn't hold the frown. He smiled and said, "Eric said I'm a goner."

"Hmmm. A seventy-year-old is calling you a

goner? As I recall, I just said I might even love you, but you didn't respond, except to dismiss my friend. Doesn't sound like you're a goner at all." Courtney's tone was light, but she was hurt. Greg didn't have a clue what her admission had meant to her, how hard it had been to tell him her feelings.

Greg stared, then took a sip of his wine. He stood, left his chair across from Courtney, and sat in the one next to her. He placed his left arm over her shoulder and his right hand in hers. "I am a goner, for sure. I love you, Courtney. You sound unsure, but I'm not. Why do you think I wanted a real date? Why else would I want you back in the office so much? I miss you all the time."

Okay, now she was feeling better. He said he loved her. But there was a smothering quality to his desire. She squeezed his hand and kissed his cheek. "Time to go back to your chair. I'm glad we've got this settled. We love each other." A tear slipped down her cheek. "But we can have real love and work apart. We want the best for each other, and the best for me is the job I have now." She kissed him again as he rose to move back across the table. "And I believe the best for you is to be focused on the clinic, without my getting in the way."

This time Greg took a large swallow of his wine, draining the glass. "We'll have to disagree on that point for now. It's not worth debating if it makes you cry."

The waiter arrived at that instant, and the rest of the time was spent eating and enjoying the sunset. After dinner, Greg asked, "What now? Am I allowed to go to your place? Do you have urgent baking to finish?" He stood and reached for her hand. "I guess I'm asking if I can be a part of the rest of your evening."

"Yes, you can," Courtney replied. "No baking or sports tonight. Just some nice music in the background while we talk."

Talking hadn't been high on Greg's list, but at least Courtney had said she "might" love him. They settled in at her condo and commenced their conversation. He was sure they were talking too much. He had other things in mind.

"Maybe if I told you about my job, it would help you understand," she said. "I so enjoy the variety and autonomy. I'm meeting lots of new people in the Destin area, which has helped my outlook. And by joining the state psychological association, I've met even more of my colleagues. It's important to me to put down some roots in Florida, since I seem to have a man in my life, one who's worth sticking around for."

Kissing her deeply, Greg finally answered, "That's good, I guess. The part about having a man to stick around for. But I still believe you're keeping me at a distance. And I think it's about the idiot from Gordon. Are you really over him, Court?"

Bouncing up from the sofa, Courtney began to pace. "Why would you say that? He's in my rearview mirror. And in case you've forgotten, he's about to be married and have a child."

"Married people have affairs all the time," Greg said quietly. "Not that I think you'd do it intentionally, but Drew sounds like a master at manipulation. I don't want just part of you, Courtney. We have to have a real commitment."

Throwing up her hands as she circled the couch for the fourth time, she exploded, "What do I have to do to convince you? I'm done with Drew. He's done with me. He humiliated me beyond belief. I'm not some masochist aching for him to come back. Nor am I a woman who would be involved with a married man. There is no happy ending to the Drew and Courtney fairytale."

Standing to block her latest lap, Greg took her in his arms. "No, you're not a masochist. But your therapy radar may be a little off. Drew is still in your heart."

"Out!" Courtney yelled. "Just leave, please. We're getting nowhere with this. Do you sense a theme here, Greg? You don't believe I love my new job. You don't believe I love you. And you don't believe I'm finished with Drew. It would appear I'm not the only one with trust issues. I'll call you later when I'm not so angry."

Greg left the beachfront building and drove home. Once again, a promising date had turned out badly. This one wasn't just bad, it was ugly. Despite that, he knew he'd hit a nerve with Courtney. Her protests had been too vehement, too excessive. Her wounds from Drew were unhealed.

Therefore, he would have to help her heal. That probably meant he needed to back off a little, something that ran counter to his usual style. He'd pursued Taryn fervently until she caught him, as the old saying went. Taryn had wanted to be captured, which was the difference between her and Courtney. Courtney wanted to be free in a relationship, however that worked. Greg understood; Drew had slowly hooked Courtney by praising her clinical skills, implying his clinic would fail without her referrals, and so forth. It was an intoxicating mix, being someone's love interest and savior. In this instance, it was also baloney.

Then he realized his part in her need for distance. She felt engulfed, trapped. It was only fair she never wanted those feelings in a relationship again. Drew had snared her in his oily need; she had to save his practice, be his lover, and please his impossible father. She was never valued for herself, just for what she could do for Drew. Could he be guilty of the same thing?

He had to admit that having Courtney in the clinic was soothing. If revenues were down, he could look to her for comfort. If no-shows were up, she could provide strategies. When patients were difficult, she had ideas for new approaches or referral options. He'd expected her to be a business partner and had rewarded her with an impossible salary cut. No wonder she wanted nothing to do with his business.

But she did want to have something to do with him. She loved her new job, but she also had feelings for him. And that was the important thing. She loved him; he knew. A woman like Courtney didn't treat love lightly, not after Dr. Drew had pierced her heart and confidence. He needed to fix all that. He'd meant to start tonight, but the evening had imploded. In large part, due to him. Bringing up Courtney's attachment to Drew had been dumb. She had to figure that piece of her life out, and he needed to back off. But in the meantime, he could court her, to use the mythical Minnie's words. Courtney would be romanced like no other woman on the Emerald Coast.

Chapter Eleven

Minnie coughed but smiled as Courtney entered the condominium. "Hello, my friend. I loved having my daughter here, but I missed you, nonetheless. I can't wait to hear what you've been up to."

After brewing their tea, the women settled into Minnie's comfortable patio lounge chairs as they watched the sky turn from pinky-purple to indigo blue. A gentle breeze softened the day's humidity and enhanced their quiet contentment. Courtney led Minnie indoors to the living area. Turning on soft jazz, the women began to catch up.

"I've been busy, but very happy," Courtney said, after Minnie filled her in on her daughter's family. "This new job is just what the doctor ordered. Bad joke, I know. But it's got variety, new people, and a good salary. I've just got to convince Greg of that."

"He'll come around," Minnie said with a wave of her hand. "Men have to think awhile, then convince themselves it was all their idea."

"Minnie, you're a very sexist lady! Men struggle just like we do." Courtney smoothed her friend's Afghan. "I know you don't hold men in so little regard."

Sending a wicked grin Courtney's way, Minnie just shrugged. "I love men, especially my dear departed Dom. I'm just saying you have to give them time."

"Fine. Anyway, I'm so grateful to God for this new job. It checks all the boxes for me. I looked in my planner at my New Year's resolutions for this year, and despite leaving the Diabetes Care Clinic, I've crossed several of my goals off the list. I'm in Destin, working a job I enjoy, and I've made lots of new friends."

"Planner, huh?" Minnie nestled into her warm blanket. "I always thought planners were overrated. They give the illusion of control, when we all know deep down there's little control in this life."

Turning to Courtney, Minnie spoke again. "I'll bet you even balance your checkbook. It's not enough for types like you to look at deposits and withdrawals, no ma'am. You probably do a complete monthly audit, to see exactly where you stand at a given moment in time. You think you've got life all settled. But life isn't perfect, though God created us that way, and we messed it up, so really, how much control do we have?"

As usual, Courtney had to think a minute about Minnie's off-brand theological take on life. Unsure about Minnie's mental status, she remembered Jessica's odd way of thinking about God and was more confused than before. "Can't we control what's in our power? Doesn't God expect us to do our best?"

"Sure, He does. But our best is more than just setting goals to make our lives better. I'll bet your resolutions didn't include sitting with an old dying lady during the last days of her life, but I think that's the most holy thing you've done this year."

Courtney's eyes filled, and despite her best efforts, the tears spilled. "Minnie, if nothing else, you've given me honesty in everything you say. I hate the thought of losing you."

"I'll be around a little longer," Minnie said. "I want to see how your love life turns out. In the meantime, I want to know if forgiving that idiot doctor in Indiana was on your resolution list."

"Uh, no, it wasn't on the list. I've forgiven him, haven't I? I've moved on."

"Two totally different things. You've moved, but you haven't moved on. He's still on your mind, isn't he? Do you find yourself wondering about him and his new wife? About their baby? About the unfairness of it all? My bet is when you get homesick, he's the one crowding your thoughts; not your sister or your friends."

Stricken, Courtney stared at the tiny lady next to her. "Minnie, that's kind of harsh. Isn't it normal to wonder about a failed relationship? My homesickness, when it hits, centers on friends and family, believe me."

Rolling her sunken eyes, Minnie chuckled. "I hope so, Courtney. I surely hope so. Now, let's get me to bed. I'm extra tired today."

Unable to sleep as Minnie's labored breathing echoed through the hallway, Courtney wondered about their conversation. Wasn't she over Drew? Was Minnie just confused and maybe a little mean? But Minnie seconded Greg's belief that she wasn't over Drew Clifton. How ironic that the two people closest to her came to the same conclusion. And Minnie seemed to think that forgiving Drew was the key to being over him.

Could they be right? Was Drew still in her heart? Her face flushed, and she was forced to admit the truth. The depth of her revulsion at Drew's actions indicated feelings of some sort. Wasn't the old truism that the opposite of love wasn't hate, it was indifference? She was not indifferent to Drew. That meant something, something she wasn't ready to admit.

Minnie (and Greg, if she were being honest) had both realized the surprising truth. Courtney's dreams of home usually started with wondering how things were going with her sister and friends, but then they wandered to Drew's status. Was he happy? Did Leslie meet his needs? Did he feel tricked or trapped by the pregnancy? Most importantly, why did Courtney care? As she'd told Greg, Drew had humiliated her in the worst way. Small-town shame was potent. People talked, shared, embellished, and then talked some more. It hit her that her musings about Gordon usually ended with Drew seeking her forgiveness and comfort, for all to see. In her fantasy life her shame was redeemed, and life went on as if nothing revolting had ever happened.

Her chest felt heavy, the weight almost rising high enough to choke her. She wanted to talk to someone, but it was too late to call Sherry. Instead, she forced herself to do what she advised her patients to do: sit with the pain, feel it deeply, and try to understand what it was trying to tell her. Several patients had initially scoffed at this "prescription", but later admitted it was worth it.

Courtney felt the pain. Deep, searing pain. Hearing the clock in Minnie's kitchen tick away, she massaged her temples, cried deep silent sobs, and wondered what she'd done to deserve such treatment from a man she'd given so much to. After a while, the tears stopped. She was exhausted but at peace. Drifting off into a light sleep, she awoke to Minnie's stooped form standing by her bunk.

"Are you okay, girl? It's after eight. You're usually up and out of here by now. Can I get you some breakfast?"

Blinking away the sleep, Courtney felt oddly refreshed. "Sure, Minnie. I'd like some cheesy scrambled eggs, cooked a little wet, with crispy bacon, grits, and an English muffin. With real butter."

Both women threw their heads back and laughed. Minnie spoke first, "Goodness, Courtney, you're full of yourself today. I'm glad to see it. Unless you're up for a stale toaster pastry, get out of here and go to work. You've got an important job. Go heal some folks."

"Not as important as the friendship you've given me, Minnie. Thanks for your tough love last night. You made several good points."

"I know. I'm a smart old woman. Too bad this culture of ours dismisses me and my peers. We'd have this world right-side-up in no time. You get going now. Don't want to lose that perfect job you've found."

Courtney went to her apartment, slurped up a high-protein yogurt smoothie, and was out the door in twenty minutes. Since she had no presentations to give, her first stop of the day was at the mood disorders clinic in the hospital. She was struck with the memory of her initial visit to the building, after Greg had paged her on her first day of work to meet Mandy and her mother. So much had changed since then! She hoped she'd grown, and due to Minnie's scolding last night, she'd begun to forgive Drew. Smiling to herself as she walked into the office portion of the hospital, she had to admit a lasting smidge of revenge fantasy. Maybe Leslie would have quadruplets, forcing the always rigid Drew to grow too!

Checking her daily roster of clients, she noted she was on admissions triage for the morning. Since this involved doing intakes with complete strangers, Courtney liked this the least of all her duties. The role forced a person to be a detective, parent, historian, and risk assessor, all in the space of sixty-minutes. But variety was the spice of her new life. She'd handle it.

Four hours later, Courtney was finished with variety. The majority of the walk-in clients had been tiring but straightforward, with one exception. Courtney went to the waiting area and saw Cathy Eller looking tense and tearful. Walking the woman back to the office, Courtney started the interview:

"Cathy, what's going on? How can I help you today?"

Mandy's mother looked concerned, shaking her head. "I'm so glad it's you, Dr. Bledsoe. I was scared of talking to a stranger, but this is okay, isn't it? Since you see Mandy in the IOP, should I be speaking to someone else?"

Wondering the same thing, Courtney made an immediate but considered decision. "Since this is a one-time intake, it's okay, Cathy. We'll talk and I'll refer you to a staff counselor other than myself. Fill me in on your concerns."

Visibly relieved, Cathy began, "I've not been sleeping, for a while now. My appetite is terrible. I'm down ten pounds, which would usually thrill me, but Mandy's noticed and that's not good given her eating disorder. I cry a lot, mostly thinking about my husband. My minister has helped me, but he said I should see someone at this clinic in case I need meds. What do you think?"

Courtney had a lot of thoughts, none of which she was ready to share. Cathy could be fully grieving the death of her husband, now that Mandy was doing well in IOP. Or there could have been marital issues that were never resolved, complicating the grief process. Or it could be something else.

"Keep talking, Cathy. I think you were smart to come here, and your minister knows you well enough to sense you needed this. What are the themes of your sad times? What do you think most about?"

"I think about disloyalty. In myself. To be honest, Mandy's dad and I never had a great marriage. We had a shotgun wedding, a detail that Mandy figured out around five years ago. We made light of it and told her we were meant to be as a couple but got started a little too soon. The point is, when Bob died I was relieved. We were more like roommates than husband and wife."

Pausing, Cathy wrinkled her brow. "When I say roommates, I mean the kind that fusses over the rent money, argues about whose turn it is to clean the bathroom, and avoids each other in general. Our marriage was based on the convenience of sharing expenses and caring for Mandy when she was diagnosed with diabetes."

"It's probably hard to grieve someone you had such mixed feelings about," Courtney said. "Do you find yourself covering up your emotions to help Mandy when she's sad about her dad?"

"That's it! I'm disloyal and I'm a hypocrite. Bob was a good father to Mandy, but I can't appreciate any of that. Pretty messed up, huh?"

"Not messed up, just conflicted. Let's book you with a therapist here who specializes in grief. She'll be a good fit for you, Cathy." After Courtney was assured that Cathy wasn't without hope, the appointment ended on a positive note. "It took guts to come in today, Cathy. Keep it up. You're a good woman and a good mom. Don't ever forget that."

As she was finishing her intake paperwork, Courtney's cell phone pinged. The text message simply said to call the hospice company caring for Minnie. Heart pounding, she dialed the number.

"Dr. Bledsoe? This is the nurse assigned to Minnie for today. I think you should come soon. She's taken a turn for the worse and asked for you. I've called her daughters, and they're making flight arrangements. Honestly, I hope they arrive in time."

"I'll get there within the hour," Courtney said. She cleared her schedule for the day and was grateful for her supervisor's understanding. Tomorrow's schedule had been blocked for online orientation modules so provided she completed them on her own time, she was free until next week.

Greg motored through his patient appointments like the driven man he was. Each person received his usual meticulous attention, but his mind focused on Courtney. He was scheduled to have dinner with his father tonight, so Eric's wisdom would again be sought.

As Greg entered his father's home, he smelled simmering garlic, onions, and peppers. "Dad, did you order a pizza? Whatever it is smells great."

Acting injured, Eric responded, "Pizza? For my only son? I think not. I ordered one of those meal kits, and you're about to taste the results. It was simple and easy to make. I decided I needed to learn to take care of myself more than I have been."

"Then what's on the menu?"

"Chicken sausage and vegetables. It's a spin on traditional Italian sausage and peppers but has much less fat. Am I healthy or what?"

Greg laughed. It was good to see his dad so light-hearted. In fact, Eric hadn't been this relaxed in quite a while. He wondered if Eric was finally moving on after his wife's death. That seemed unlikely, since his dad was cooking his own meals. It was time, but Greg also wondered what he'd do if his father came home with another woman. That would be tough for him, but his dad's happiness was his ultimate goal.

After a rich but heart-friendly dinner, Greg asked his pressing question, "Dad, I've got a situation with Courtney. I need your input. She loves her new job. I miss her at the clinic. She insists she's over the guy in Indiana, but I don't believe her. So, I need help with getting her to realize we were meant to be together, and that we should work together as well. What do you think?"

"I think your analysis is flawed," Eric said as he sipped his wine. "If you love Courtney, and I know you do, you'll want the best for her. If the new job is her choice, you need to accept it." Eric smiled at Greg. "To be honest, son, the two of you were not meant to work together. Professionally, I mean. As a couple I think you'd work just fine."

"How can you say that, Dad? I need her at the clinic. She's smart, great with patients, and the staff all love her. She helps me when I'm stuck – both with tough patients and with administrative stuff. Why should she have to establish herself at a new place if she's got a spot at the Diabetes Care Clinic? You know this. You hired her, after all!"

"Sounds like we're talking about you, not Courtney," Eric said. "In fact, you sound like the man she just ended things with. Didn't he want Courtney to ensure the success of his business at the expense of their relationship? Time to grow up, Greg."

Greg sputtered, barely able to get his words out. "Grow up? I'm pretty grown, last I checked. Dad, how can you possibly compare me to Dr. Sleaze? I respect Courtney far too much to want to use her like he did."

Eric was cool. "Let's see. Dr. Sleaze, as you call him, wanted Courtney for her ability to help his business. Ditto for you. He wanted to romance her, until he found a more useful woman. You're on tricky ground here, son."

Stunned, Greg stood. "It's been a good evening, Dad. But I've got to go. Thanks for your insight. I'm not sure I agree, but I'll consider what you've said."

Not in this lifetime, Dad. You're wrong about me. I love Courtney for herself, not for what she can do for me. Red faced and breathing hard, Greg unlocked his car, then stood still. Was he protesting too much? His dad had hit a nerve.

Courtney entered Minnie's condo and was immediately hushed by the hospice aide. Whispering, she cautioned, "Minnie's finally sleeping. Her daughters will land at midnight. Can you stay until then? I have to get to another patient's home."

"Sure," Courtney said. "Is there anything I should know about her care?"

"No, Miss Minnie has a pain pump and knows about her oxygen settings. If she wakes up, you're the best medicine she can have. She's told me often how much comfort you are to her."

Still anxious despite the aide's words, Courtney made a cup of tea. She turned on the television and was soon disheartened by the offerings. If she saw another reality show, she'd choke. True reality involved situations like the one she was currently in, not fake engagements or marrying without meeting the person until the ceremony.

Chuckling to herself, she had to admit that given her own romantic history, maybe an arranged marriage was what she needed. No need to figure out who was "the one", but instead just take whoever was at the altar. Shaking her head, she let out an involuntary, "Nope!"

Sipping her tea, she turned to the music station. Finding some gentle jazz, she prayed for her friend. *Lord, Minnie has led a good life, one devoted to You and to her family. Please cover her with your protection as she enters into your kingdom. Please allow her daughters to arrive for their loving farewells. And thank You for leading us to be friends.*

Feeling better, Courtney stepped out to Minnie's

balcony. Watching the waves added to her feelings of peace. When all was said and done, life amounted to just this. We were all destined to leave this world and meet our Maker. In the meantime, life was meant to be lived with God at our center while loving those around us.

She realized she'd have to love Greg into realizing they were meant to be together, just not nine to five. Love was the ultimate persuasion, right? God would help her, she knew.

"Is anyone here?" the feeble voice asked from the bedroom.

"I'm here, Minnie," Courtney said as she rushed to Minnie's bedside. "What can I do for you?"

"Just sit with me," Minnie said. "I'm not nearly as bad as they say, girl. I hear my daughters are on their way. I feel bad about that, what with all the cost and disruption to their families and jobs. Those hospice folks don't know so much. I've got lots of time left."

They know enough, Courtney thought. She was taken aback by the change in Minnie since she'd last seen her. Her friend's color was gray, and her hands had a distinct tremor. "How about some tea?" Courtney asked. "I bought some new blackberry almond flavor for us to try."

"That sounds awful," Minnie crabbed. "Just stick with Earl Gray for me. I don't need any of that designer beverage silliness."

Laughing after she made Minnie's drink, Courtney teased, "Well, you sure sound good, Minnie, as cantankerous as ever. If you're up to it, I'd rather hear about your love life. You've certainly heard enough about my silly history."

Minnie's eyes sparkled. "My Dominic was no

fairytale prince. He wouldn't go to church, swore like a sailor on leave, and was short, dark, and not very handsome." She breathed slowly, as if the memories held comfort. "No, he wouldn't have made the cut for a modern happily-ever-after. But he was smart and sexy. He knew how to treat his wife and later his daughters, though they often argued about what they should major in at college. Dom always told them to choose something 'suitable for a woman'. That riled them up, for sure!"

"But he was an old school Italian male," she continued. "He loved them so much and wanted everything for them. To his way of thinking, women were best suited for teaching or nursing. Funny, huh? Fortunately, neither of his daughters listened, and no one was prouder than Dom when they got their graduate degrees."

Courtney sipped her exotic tea and reflected on Minnie's words. "But Minnie, you're such a spitfire. How did you and Dominic make a go of it? There must have been some spirited *discussions*."

Unable to sustain a giggle, Minnie answered, "Discussions, huh? I guess so. But over time, we learned to appreciate the other's strengths. Isn't that the current big thing? Not focusing on weaknesses, but strengths?"

"Maybe, but you're avoiding the issue. How did you and Dominic come to terms in a loving way?"

"As I told you before, men need time. And sometimes a little manipulation doesn't hurt the cause. As the years passed, and when the girls came along, Dominic needed me more than before and he realized it, which was the crucial thing. Once the kids were in school, we were able to work together as full partners in the business. I tracked the office details and the money, so Dom was able to devote his efforts to managing the workers and the customers. We had some terrific fights, and usually I was right. I could read people. I knew when a hire wasn't going to work out. Eventually he trusted my judgment in pretty much all of the business dealings. Did I ever tell you about the best present he ever got me?"

Imagining sparkling diamonds or a cruise around the world, Courtney shook her head.

"On our fortieth anniversary, he presented me with one of those legal piles of paperwork with the blue cover. It was a document changing the name of the company to 'M and D Construction'. Get it? Not only was my initial on the company name, but it was first." Minnie swiped a tear but smiled at the memory.

"That's such a sweet tribute," Courtney said, getting weepy herself. "But not only sweet, but an acknowledgement of all you'd done for him and for your family." Patting Minnie's veiny hand, she continued, "Your story has just become my goal for a marriage. I want to be a true partner with my husband. To paraphrase Disney, 'Someday my true and equal partner will come'."

Minnie drifted off with the smile etched in her face. Courtney heard a text ping in the other room. Reading it, she breathed a relieved sigh. Minnie's daughters had just landed. They would arrive at Miramar Beach within the hour.

Thank you, Lord. The family can reunite. Minnie won't be alone, and neither will I.

Chapter Twelve

Greg called the mood disorders clinic and learned Courtney was out until next week; something about a family emergency. He knew the family member in question was probably Minnie and was determined to give Courtney the space she needed to comfort her friend.

He also knew Minnie's death, which might be coming sooner than he'd thought, would affect Courtney in ways she couldn't fathom. Her grief about her parents was bound to resurface, as would her sense of loss from Dr. Sleaze. Greg was determined to be there for her, for the woman he loved.

Hating his father's wisdom at the same time he was admitting the truth in it, he also determined to be the exact opposite of Drew. Courtney would have her space in all things, not just in comforting her friend. Her professional life was hers, not his. As long as she was his life partner, he would be content. Eric had certainly drilled that idea home, with the finesse of a battering ram. Greg had been selfish with all his relationships, not just with Courtney.

He'd thought he was different this time, since he wasn't after frequent booty calls, but he was selfish in a more damaging way. He'd wanted Courtney to satisfy his professional needs as well as his personal desires, although he'd sure like to have her satisfy other needs as well. All in good time.

As he was about to drift off, his cell phone rang. Who would call now? If it was medically related, he'd get a page. Seeing Courtney's name on the screen, he answered quickly.

"Greg? Are you there?"

"I'm here, Court. Are you okay? You sound sniffly." He heard a sound that combined a laugh and a wail.

"Sniffly. Is that a new medical term?" Courtney asked. "But to answer your question, I'm not okay, but I will be. Minnie just died. I was honored to be there with her daughters when she passed. They all insisted I stay. But I'm okay."

Greg didn't hesitate. "I'm coming over right now. If you don't want my company, I'll camp out in the lobby of your building. You shouldn't be alone, Courtney. Minnie meant a lot to you."

"Thanks," Courtney whispered. "You don't have to stay in the lobby."

Greg's car flew over the roads to Miramar Beach. The lights were well-coordinated at this late hour, for which he thanked God. Courtney's door opened as he approached, and she grabbed him in an almost painful hug. Making his way inside, they sat close on her sofa. Then her tears began.

After five full minutes of sobbing, Courtney looked up at him. "You're a good man, Dr. Greg McClure. I needed you and you came. Thank you for that. I owe you."

"You owe me nothing," he protested. "What's a guy to do when the woman he loves is in pain? Ignore it until it's daytime?"

Smiling through her tears, Courtney kissed him tenderly. "That's one of the many reasons I love you back, Greg." She shifted on the couch so that she was nestled in his arms, both of them half reclining. "Now that you've seen what an ugly crier I am, I'm going to rest a bit. Help yourself to whatever you'd like in the kitchen. There are fresh cheese biscuits. I know you like them."

Determined not to move until Courtney was awake, Greg held her closer. She'd called him when she'd been lost and alone. She'd said she loved him and pointed out there were many reasons for that emotion. Despite his anguish at her sorrow, he was a happy man.

Courtney opened her eyes and tried to move her stiff legs. They were tangled in something. She also noticed a warmth enveloping her body, but the Afghan was still draped over the top of the couch. Looking up, she saw Greg's eyes studying her.

"Now I remember," she said. "You helped me so much last night. Thanks again for coming. I couldn't believe how Minnie's death affected me. I cried more than her daughters, so much so that they sent me home and insisted I call a friend."

"A friend?" Greg's eyes weren't as welcoming as they had been a minute before. "You said you loved me, Court. Are we going to have another fight about what constitutes friendship?"

"No, no fighting today," Courtney said as she put

her arms around Greg's neck, placing her body almost entirely on top of his. "The best relationships begin with friendship, haven't you heard? I want a man with the whole package." Scowling at Greg's lecherous grin, she punched him lightly on the arm. "The package I'm referring to is one of emotional depth. You've got it, Greg, despite what you pretend. You're not that bad boy who was involved with the woman Jackie detested. I'm very grateful to have you in my life."

"That goes both ways," Greg said. "But, Court, I'm surprised that you're surprised at your grief for Minnie. You two were close." He stopped as if he were wondering whether to continue. "And grief can be about lots of things. Your mom and dad, moving here away from all you knew in Indiana, and..."

Feeling chilled, Courtney sat up, nearly toppling Greg to the floor. Good thing her second-hand sofa sat low. "You mean Drew, don't you? I guess you're right, but I don't want to think about him right now. Minnie's death seems too pure, her spirit too full of goodness, to contaminate my thoughts with Drew." Kissing Greg lightly on the cheek, she said, "And Minnie was a fan of yours, by the way. I'll have to see if her predictions come true."

Intrigued, Greg began to hammer her with questions. "She was my fan? What specifically did she like about me? What did you tell her? Did you two discuss my genius-level intelligence, my good looks, or my tremendous skill in both medicine and business?"

Moving to the kitchen, Courtney continued the kidding, "She said one of her friends from church spoke highly of your treatment of her diabetes. Other than that, Minnie didn't have much to say about you. What would you like for breakfast? Scones? Belgian waffles?"

Greg followed her as she began to set out pans and dishes. "Nothing that elaborate. Coffee will suffice. What do you usually have for breakfast after a tough night?"

Kissing him again, Courtney marveled at the man in front of her. "I usually have whatever my intuition suggests. I don't do a regimented diet thing. Most days it's coffee, like you, plus some sort of decent protein. I was teasing about scones and waffles. Would you like some eggs?"

"Perfect," Greg said as he sat on the stool at her bar. "Can I help?"

"Just pour me a cup of java. It's almost finished. In the meantime, I'll scramble us some eggs with my usual fixings."

Later as he scooted back from the bar, Greg patted his belly. "I'll have to work out extra after this feast," he said. "What's your secret to cooking the eggs so they're moist without being underdone? And the mix of cheeses was perfect."

"Maybe someday I'll tell you," Courtney said. "In the meantime, don't you have to get to the clinic? I've got some time off until next week, but I'm betting you're booked solid." *And I'll have other things to do,* she thought. *Minnie's daughters might need help with her memorial.*

As if he read her mind, Greg took her in his arms again. "I'll send up a prayer for you three today. I know it's hard to lose a person like Minnie. Do you want me to stop by tonight? I can bring dinner if that would help."

"Yes, please stop by. But just bring yourself. I'll cook for us tonight. Oddly enough, cooking helps me relax and my guess is I'll need to wind down after time spent at the funeral home."

Courtney sipped a glass of wine while she planned dinner for Greg. The day had been draining but not terrible. Minnie's plans for her memorial service in Fort Wayne were quite detailed, so her daughters simply had to arrange for the transfer of the body to Indiana. The three women spent much of the morning reminiscing about Minnie, both her foibles and strong personality. Her daughters were emphatic that Courtney had been treated to Minnie's best, in contrast to her strict and sometimes unpleasant, parenting style with them. Laughter punctuated the tears, with the threesome ending their day's work around noon.

Munching on a tuna salad sandwich, Courtney reflected on the complexities of life. Minnie had been a demanding mom, but a sweet friend to her. She realized Minnie was difficult at times with her as well, calling her "girl" when she wanted to send some tough love. Courtney sent up a prayer of thanks, for old and new friends, and for the comfort God seemed to be sending just when she needed it.

After a quick shower and a change into a swirly skirt with a tank top, Courtney commenced cooking. Roast chicken, whipped potatoes with pan gravy, cornbread stuffing, fresh green beans, and biscuits seemed like a comforting meal. Strawberry parfait for dessert lightened the potential calorie count a bit. Just as she finished setting the table, her doorbell chimed.

"What's that glorious smell?" Greg asked. "I'd swear it was Thanksgiving in here." Accepting his glass of wine, he kissed Courtney lightly on the cheek. "Really, Court, you didn't have to go to any trouble."

"This is what *friends* do for each other," she bantered. "It wasn't any trouble. As I've told you, cooking and baking help me relax."

Deep into the meal, while taking a second helping of the stuffing, Greg rolled his eyes. "This is great. What mix did you use for this?"

Giving him the evil eye, Courtney answered with false anger. "Mix? What is this mix you speak of? I baked a loaf of cornbread, crumbled it, and added all the other ingredients. No need to be insulting, mister!"

They laughed, and Greg explained, "My mom was the queen of taking convenience foods and jazzing them up so they tasted homemade. I meant no offense by my question. One time she served a stuffing that had chopped pecans, bits of sausage, and diced onions that everyone raved over. It took a shaming look from my father to make her admit it was a box mix that she'd doctored up with a few leftover savory items." Greg smiled at the memory of his parents' jousting. "Then the next Thanksgiving, she did the same thing, only with dried cranberries and golden raisins. Dad knew better than to question her recipe."

Smiling at Greg's enjoyment of his memories of his family, Courtney added to the mix, "My mother was a good cook, but like yours, she took help wherever she could get it. Mostly that meant that I peeled lots of potatoes, while Sherry scraped and diced carrots. For other meals, we made homemade yeast rolls, twice-baked potatoes, and even some of the simpler casseroles. You get the picture. Mom got lots of kudos for her cooking, but Dad and our guests had no idea what an extensive kitchen staff she had." Courtney wiped a tear. "But I'm not complaining. Sherry and I learned how to keep house, which is an old-fashioned way of saying that we learned to take care of ourselves. I think now it's called 'adulting'. And don't get me started on my ability to iron a man's dress shirt."

Drawing her into his arms, Greg said, "How about a sunset walk on the beach? We can clean up after we get back."

"No, guests do not clean up. I'll get to it soon enough, either tonight or tomorrow. As I've told you I've got some time off, but you do not. Let's get that walk in before the sun goes down."

Holding her hand as they navigated the other walkers, Greg cleared his throat. "I've been wanting to say this for a while, Court. You were right about us each having our own careers. I miss you like crazy at the office, but the new psychologist is doing good work. And you seem so happy with your new position. God finally got my attention, with a little help from my dad, and as long as I can see you a lot, let's stick with the status quo."

It was Courtney's turn to roll her eyes, which Greg couldn't see in the partial light of dusk. "It sounds like you're giving me permission to work where I want. Or that you've found a better psychologist and are easing out of my returning to the

Diabetes Care Clinic. Which is it?"

"Neither, and you know better. I do miss our fussing about patients; the new guy is way too calm when we disagree. However, remember I said I need to see you a lot. What's your response to that?"

"My response is that I agree. Obviously, I work a few evenings at the IOP, but otherwise, I want to be with you, too." Looking down, she said quietly, "After all, we do love each other, right?"

Greg's answer was to stop mid stride, nearly causing a collision with the power-walker behind them, and to envelop her in a bear hug. Kissing her with a passion that resulted in a few wolf whistles from those lounging in beach chairs, he said, "You bet we love each other, Dr. Bledsoe. Since we won't be fussing at work, we'll have to figure out a way to fuss and make up on our own time."

"Or we don't need to fuss at all," Courtney said with a smirk. "We can just make up whenever we want."

Courtney adjusted slowly to Minnie's death, more so to the lack of the woman's presence in her life. She missed the free advice, the spin on life's challenges, and above all, Minnie's deep faith that life was worth living and that things would work out eventually.

She also admitted that Minnie's wisdom about Drew had been spot on. Courtney often found herself imagining her life with Greg instead of wondering what Drew's life was like now. She even found herself laughing at some of Drew's blatant manipulations, ones she'd ignored like the besotted woman she had been. Comparing Greg to Drew (didn't she advise against the comparison trap during her IOP sessions?), she marveled at their differences. Previously she'd been sure they were alike in their determination to grow their clinics, but now she knew how wrong she'd been. Drew was determined all right, to the extent that his ethics had left him. Greg, on the other hand, was able to listen when his father confronted his selfishness. And that was the other sad piece of Drew's life – his father, Dan Clifton, didn't actually want the best for him, just the best for his own community image.

As she prepped leftovers from her "Thanksgiving" dinner with Greg, Courtney's phone sent its traditional ring. She almost dropped the bowl of green beans when she saw Drew's name on the caller ID. Was God playing a joke on her? Hadn't she just put Drew out of her thoughts? She'd even forgiven him for his weakness and said a prayer that he find happiness with his new family!

"Hello?" she answered, hoping the call was a mistake, hoping that Drew had changed his number.

"Courtney? It's Drew. How are you doing?"

"I'm fine. Just in the middle of my supper. What's up?"

Drew had the awareness to pause, as if sending the message that his call wasn't entirely out of line and that Courtney was being curt. "I wanted to see you, Court. I'm in town, in Destin actually, just a few minutes from your place. Do you have any time to meet?"

Courtney opened the refrigerator door and leaned into the soothing cool air. What did this guy want from her? How could he dare ask to meet? Sucking in the faint odor of onions and butter, she closed the door and answered. "I can't imagine what we've got to say that would require a meeting, Drew. Why don't we just chat on the phone?"

"No, I need to see you," he said. Courtney was reminded of his stubborn, single-minded manner. Six months ago, she'd labeled it a personality strength. Now the difference was clear. Egocentric and selfish.

"I can be at your condo in thirty minutes," Drew continued.

Angry that Drew had the gall to have looked up her address and then invited himself over, she put a stop to that plan. "I'll meet you on the beach. There's a little restaurant on the sand, to the west of my building. I'll be in front." She gave him the restaurant's name and hung up before Drew could protest. There was no way she was letting him into her unit. Her condo was her sanctuary; just letting Drew see it was too invasive. He didn't have the right to view the new life she'd built for herself. And she realized her home was meant to host Greg, but never Drew.

Appetite gone, she took an insulated cup of sweet tea down to the beach and waited. She greeted the owner of the restaurant and waved to familiar faces walking the hard sand. Drew arrived in barely twenty minutes. Either he'd been graced by the traffic gods, or he'd driven too fast.

"Courtney, honey, it's so nice to see you. Looking great, as always, though you've got a Floridian tan, despite your fair skin. Life must be good."

She stared and arched a brow. Drew was playing a consistent game, which was yet another realization she'd ignored in the past. He combined a compliment with a subtle dig, then added praise which almost demanded an explanation. As in, tell me what's going on in your life.

Determined to maintain her poise, she smiled. "Life is good, Drew. And I hope yours is too. What are you doing in the Destin area?"

Having the grace to redden, Drew looked away. "Actually, I'm here on my honeymoon. Or, in the vernacular of the younger set, my babymoon. Leslie's at the spa, having the full day treatment."

Courtney waited for Drew's next statement. He wasn't going to throw her with talk of honeymoons. Or babymoons. What a creep. Or sleaze, as Greg referred to him.

"Well, we need to talk, Court. Or I guess I do. It's important to me that I have your forgiveness. What I did was wrong though if you admit the truth, we were pretty much over. Leslie got me, you know? She understood how important my clinic was to me. You never really did. I'd ask for referrals, and you were very slow with them. We weren't a team."

If Courtney's brows arched any higher, she'd have a stroke. But God was with her, allowing her to remain quiet. Until Drew's next statement.

"And my dad knew it from the start. Courtney. You weren't on my side. Your allegiance was always to GCC, to the students, no matter what I needed. How were we supposed to build a life with those differences?"

Taking a deep breath, Courtney truly wanted to slap Drew silly. Again, God calmed her. Smiling full on now, she said, "You're right, Drew. We wanted different things. But you seemed to have wasted a trip. There's no need for my forgiveness. You've had it for a long time now." Though she had just recently truly forgiven Drew, Courtney asked God to let that little white lie go.

"But forgiveness is a tricky thing," she continued. "I'll bet *Leslie's* the woman you should be asking for forgiveness. She doesn't know you're here, does she? What did you tell her – that you needed a long walk? That you wanted to buy her a surprise at the outlet mall?"

Asking God for His forbearance, Courtney went on, "As I consider your usual style, Drew, you should really be asking Leslie to forgive you for all the lies you've told her since you've been together. Today's trip to see me can't possibly be your first fib. I'm sure you and your father consult regularly about her suitability to raise a child, how it should be educated, where the holidays will be spent, all the little things a man should talk to his wife about. But that's not how you and Dan roll, is it?"

Running his hands through his hair, which Courtney was sure had thinned considerably since her arrival in Florida, Drew shot back, "Leslie and I don't have any secrets. I told her where I was going."

Finally knowing a lie when she heard it, Courtney pulled out her phone. "That's great, Drew! Let me give her a call and say hi. I can give her some good shopping recommendations, too. I've got her number in my contact list from GCC. It won't take a second."

Pulling her arm away from her ear, Drew sighed. "Fine. You win. I guess we're done here."

"Oh, we've been done for a long time," Courtney said, turning on her heel toward her building.

Chapter Thirteen

After a perfect meal of leftovers, Courtney marveled at her peace of mind. She'd seen Drew, confronted him with his treachery, and it felt wonderful. She was free, finally. Suddenly there was no pull to return to Indiana, to try to salvage a remnant of the innocent life she'd thought she had. Sure, she missed Sherry and her other friends, but she had a full life in Florida. Even if she and Greg were to implode and end their relationship, she would be fine with Destin as her home. What a difference a few months made!

Her phone rang, and she smiled at Greg's name on the ID. "Hi, good looking!" she answered. "It's a pleasure to hear your voice."

Greg chuckled and asked, "I must have the wrong number. I was calling Dr. Bledsoe, a very professional woman. She never answers the phone like that."

"I'm in a terrific mood, Greg. You'll never guess why."

"Well, I know you're headed back to work in a few days, but that doesn't seem like a reason to blatantly flirt before you're even sure it's me on the line." He paused, pretending to ponder. "Could it be you were about to call me? Certainly, that would have put you in a fine mood, just thinking about my good looks. Am I right?"

"No, not even close," Courtney said. "I'm in a great mood because I just received a visit from Drew Clifton. What do you say to that?"

"I say it's not at all funny, Courtney. That creep can't be in Florida, can he?"

"Yes, the creep is staying with his new wife in Destin for a holiday before the baby comes. It doesn't matter, Greg. He wanted my forgiveness but in a half-hearted way, almost in the hopes I'd be devastated by his presence."

Courtney heard Greg gulp. "Surely you weren't devastated. What did you say to him?"

"I said quite a mouthful, my dearest. In essence, I told Drew I was onto his self-serving lies. Would you believe Leslie didn't even know he was meeting me?"

"Sure, I'd believe it," Greg grunted. "Men like that always want to keep their options open for the future. Women are a commodity, one or two to be kept in reserve just in case. He wanted to make sure you were still in his camp should he ever tire of his new wife." After another gulp, he said, "And I'm ashamed to admit I was that sort of man in the past. It's important I own that, instead of being full of righteous indignation about Drew."

"Boy, I love you," Courtney sighed. "That's the most romantic thing you've ever said to me."

"Go figure. I can't believe my sorry admission counts as romantic talk. You're a confusing woman, Courtney Bledsoe. In any event, I want to see you soon. We have lots of planning to do."

"We have plenty of time for plans," Courtney said. "I'm headed to work in a couple of days, and I need to get organized before that. I can fit you in for Sunday brunch. Would that work?"

"Brunch?" Greg groaned. "I thought we were past those stuffy, touristy Sunday time-wasters. I want to hang out with you for the whole day."

Pretending to be put-upon, Courtney said, "Fine. I'll do all my chores on Saturday, so Sunday is yours. What did you have in mind?"

"I had in mind to spend the day with the woman I love," he answered with a distinct edge. "I'll be by your place on Sunday at ten. Dress casually and bring a bathing suit and towel."

"Bossy, aren't we?" Courtney had to smile. Greg was easy to tease when he missed her. She thanked God for sending this man into her life. Fingers crossed that Greg would turn out to be as wonderful as she hoped.

Saturday was spent cleaning the condo from top to bottom. Courtney was glad she'd started with the bathroom, her least favorite job in the world. She was also grateful she'd bought a small place. Cleaning didn't take much time at all. She'd have a few hours to bake something for Greg's mysterious Sunday adventure. Maybe muffins. Or lemon bars. And she'd put together some pimento cheese sandwiches. He'd implied they'd be at the beach, so finger foods were good choices.

Answering her phone, she was cheered by Jessica's voice. "What are you up to, Courtney? I miss you, and since *you've* not bothered to call *me*, I'm taking the initiative. When can we meet for lunch?"

"Well, as you know, I'm very busy and booked out for weeks," Courtney joked. "As it happens, I can fit you in today. Tomorrow is taken."

"I'll wager I know who's booked you for tomorrow," Jessica said. "Dr. McClure has been on a real roller coaster lately. We take bets on whether he's seen enough of you or if he'll be grouchy until you two have another date."

"I'm sure his mood has nothing to do with me. So, are you up for lunch today or not?"

"Sure am. And shopping, too. I need to update my wardrobe. I've been feeling
shabby."

Laughing at the thought of Jessica being even remotely shabby, Courtney agreed.

"Let's meet at the mall and eat at the vegan place. I've been slacking off on my vegetable intake lately."

"I'm the dietitian here, remember? And if I'm paying big bucks for a meal out, it's not going to be for veggies. I'm making an executive decision. We're eating at the steakhouse adjacent to the mall. You can order a sad salad if you want, but I'm getting a filet."

"Yes, ma'am," Courtney said, as she gave Jessica a salute over the phone feed. "See you in an hour."

Later, Jessica chewed her bite of tender steak and swooned. "This is so good," she whispered. "No fancy sauce needed for meat this special. Just melted butter, and lots of it."

Munching on her salad, albeit with strips of steak and chunks of bleu cheese scattered across the lettuce, Courtney smiled. "Thanks so much for calling, Jess. My friend died, and I've been all over the map mood wise. Sad about her, but happy that Greg and

I are in a good place, finally."

"Yes, he said you'd lost your neighbor. That's big. She was your first real friend when you moved here, right?"

"True. But her suffering ended, and God took care of her and her loved ones. I'm full of gratitude for that."

"And you don't need to fill me in on you and Dr. M. It's obvious you both figured

things out. Took long enough."

"We were a little slow, weren't we? But trust is tough, Jessica. I've done the whole forgiveness thing with Drew, but even now it's tough to trust Greg entirely."

Jessica sipped her water, and grimaced. "I guess you needed to forgive Dr. Sleaze as much for yourself as for him. Not that he deserved it. But remember that forgiveness and trust are two sides of the same coin." She looked at Courtney with meaning.

Having no idea what her buddy was getting at, Courtney shrugged. "Listen, I can forgive Drew, but there's no way I'd ever trust him again. Can you believe he showed up here and didn't tell his new *pregnant* wife he was sneaking out to see me? There's a difference between trust and stupidity, Jess."

"He's slime," Jessica agreed, savoring another bite of tenderloin. "You're missing my point, though. After you've forgiven scum like him, you have to trust the world again. You need to trust God that all men aren't like Drew. If you can't trust that there are fine, good men still around, your life is pretty much a script in a bad movie. You want more out of this life, don't you?"

Courtney nodded, and Jessica used this as her cue

to continue. "What kind of limp excuse for a woman would you be if you let lowlifes like Drew color your world for the rest of your time on earth? Please, woman, you need to get tough. There's love to be had, and you know it. Quit this tentative approach to romance. It's time to embrace it." She leered at Courtney. "And I mean the word 'embrace' both literally and figuratively, my friend."

Courtney looked away. Jessica had a point, as usual. When would she give Greg a real chance? She was almost playing at loving him, while waiting for him to do something she'd mark as a betrayal. "You're right, Jess. All I can say is I'm trying. But Drew did a number on me. How do you get past that? I thought things were going well, at least until the end."

"No, you didn't," Jessica said between bites of bread dipped in the buttery steak drippings. "You pretended things were good. Admit it. Drew gave you plenty of hints, didn't he?"

Thinking back, Courtney studied the cream-colored linen cloth. "I guess he did. More accurately, he would talk about his father's reaction to my 'stingy' referral tallies. Or his dad's concern about my focus on my work, instead of being with Drew every evening. And that I'd be a distracted mother when we had kids if I was still on call for the college. Drew was never the bad guy, and I let him get away with that."

"Well, Dr. Eric loves you, so there are no daddy issues with Greg. Get the lead out and commit already," Jessica said. "Your antennae are well-tuned to Greg's feelings. I doubt you're getting any signals that he's dissatisfied or interested in anyone else."

"That's true. He seems pretty happy that we're together."

"Thank the stars in heaven for that," Jessica said as she picked up the dessert menu. "The office atmosphere can't take much more of his mood swings."

Greg studied the website for the cruise company located on the Destin Harbor Boardwalk. A snorkeling cruise, followed by a luxury dinner on land, and capped by the sunset cruise would make the perfect day for him and Courtney. It was time he romanced the woman, and hard. Their lives had been too full of complications lately. He missed her and wanted her in his life. All the time.

Courtney met him at her door, carrying a bag full of the items he'd ordered her to bring, but a lot more from the looks of the stuffed tote. "That seems pretty full for a bathing suit and towel," he grumbled. "We're not traveling abroad, you know. It's just a day's outing."

"Well, we have to eat," Courtney said. "I've got lots of finger foods in here."

"As if I wouldn't feed you?" He kissed her soundly and led her to his car. "You smell great," he said, savoring her latest perfume. "Every day is different with you. I think it's a trick you play on us poor, clueless men. We're used to women having a signature scent."

"It's nothing that devious. It's more a matter of buying perfumes on sale, usually in small sample sizes. I never get bored, and if something doesn't suit me, I'm not out a lot of money." Looking at Greg as he pulled out of the parking space, she asked, "What's our agenda today? I assume we'll be in the ocean, but that's all I've got."

"I decided it's time you got to know your new hometown," Greg said. "All you ever do is work and tend to others. Today is about fun, learning some of the leisure options available to you, and of course, spending quality time with a certain good-looking guy."

After twenty-five minutes of negotiating Destin's weekend traffic, they arrived at the cruise office. Greg decided it was time to tell the day's secret. "We will have an afternoon snorkel cruise, coolers welcome so your food won't go to waste, then dinner at a great restaurant, and then a sunset cruise. What do you think?"

"Sounds lovely," Courtney said, with a trace of anxiety in her tone. "Is it hard to snorkel? Indiana's strip pits offered lots of murky green water and a few sunken school buses, but no pretty marine life."

"Strip pits? What kind of woman am I with? Are you telling me you skinny-dipped when you went out for a summer's day of fun? Did you ever do such things with Dr. Drew?" He was only half kidding. Drew's surprise visit still rankled. What kind of history did he and Courtney share?

"Strip *pits*, silly. Not strip swimming. Strip pits are the lakes that result after strip or surface mining. Indiana has lots of them. And how dare you think I'd skinny dip? Really!"

Suitably chastised, Greg did some damage control. "Sorry. I just don't know the Indiana jargon. And I'm an idiot to think you'd bare all swimming with Drew. To address your question, snorkeling is easy. You just breathe through your mouth and enjoy the scenery. If you get scared, you can lift your head and you're open to the fresh air. But after a little practice, you'll love keeping your face in the water as the fish and other wildlife swim by."

Obviously doubtful, Courtney seemed determined to be brave. He loved that about her. Always ready for a new experience. Well, unlike Dr. Sleaze, he wouldn't steer her wrong. She would love snorkeling as much as he did.

Greg's predictions proved accurate. After just a few mild choking episodes, Courtney became an expert at sighting all the schools of colorful fish. She even spotted an eel half hidden behind a rock. He was inordinately proud of her, as if her enjoyment of the ocean signaled she was meant to be his. He was lost over this woman.

After changing and doing some window shopping, he suggested dinner. "I know it's a little early, but we have to be back on the boat for the sunset cruise. Could you eat again after all the snacking we did on your sandwiches and sweets?"

"I can almost always eat," Courtney assured him. "Let's go."

Dinner was another treat for Greg. Courtney raved over the fresh grouper and the Key Lime pie. As she was savoring her last bite, Greg ruined the mood. Intentionally.

"How are you doing now that you've had a chance to interpret Drew's visit? Any new thoughts about his making such an effort to see you?" He looked at her expectantly, regretting the flare of anger he saw in her eyes.

"I told you, Greg. Drew means nothing to me. And Jessica set me right on a few things I ignored about that relationship." Courtney swallowed a large drink of tea. "My new worry is that you're a jealous, possessive type. There's no winning with men like that, so 'fess up if that's your nature. I need to know now."

"Jealous type? I've never been accused of that before. The opposite, actually." The women in his life often complained about his emotional distance, his lack of regard about their comings and goings between his calls. He shrugged and traced her lips with his finger. "I just love you. I hate that Drew would impose his manipulations on your new life. That's all, believe me."

"Okay, but I'm going to keep an eye on you," Courtney said. She smiled and added, "I love you, too."

They made their way back to the boat and settled in on the top deck. Greg bought an overpriced bottle of sparkling wine and they enjoyed nature's spectacular show. The colorful, almost moody sunset was enhanced by the cloudless sky and shimmering water. An hour later, they waited their turn to disembark.

Greg looked down at a couple leaving, or trying to leave, the boat. The woman was having trouble with her balance, small wonder given her bulk and swollen ankles. Courtney noticed them at the same time. Her startled eyes, blushing cheeks, and rapid blinking told him all he needed to know. Dr. Sleaze had taken his wife on the sunset cruise. And based on what Greg had gleaned about Courtney and Drew's history together, his wife's pregnancy was quite a lot farther along than expected. He took Courtney's hand, squeezed it, and kissed her temple.

"It's okay, Court. I'm here for you. I love you."

"I love you, too," she said. "Let's go say hi to a couple of my old friends."

Greg studied Courtney carefully. Her eyes were clear, and she had a calm but fierce look. She was fine. But she was also intent on capturing Drew before he left the dock.

"Drew, honey, is that you?" Courtney was playing the part of an old acquaintance to perfection. "Wait up. I want to say hi to you and Leslie."

Uncertain of how the charade would play out, Greg decided to follow Courtney's lead. She guided him through the crush of people, which was helping Courtney's cause by preventing Drew from scurrying off the boat. Of course, his wife's size was also hindering his efforts.

"There you two are!" Courtney called out. "It's so good to see faces from home. How are you doing, Leslie?"

The young woman smiled, but her eyes were guarded. "I'm good, Courtney. Not graceful, but good. We're in town for our honeymoon. The baby's going to keep us close to home soon."

Drew looked sweaty, which Greg enjoyed. This guy had dragged his pregnant, and probably clueless, wife down to Destin so he could talk to Courtney. Based on Leslie's size, she had no business traveling so far. Flying was not recommended for a woman at her stage of pregnancy, and the alternative long road trip had to be agony in terms of bathroom breaks. And those puffy ankles! What kind of doctor was Drew, if he didn't know this stuff? Oh right, he was Dr. Sleaze.

Greg continued to watch Courtney's little play. He nearly stumbled as he saw her hug Leslie. "Yes, you're going to be very busy soon, Leslie. That little one will be here any day. I can't believe Drew let you travel at this point in your pregnancy."

"I told her she'd be fine," Drew said. "Her OB gave her the go ahead."

Frowning, Leslie interjected. "He wasn't totally on board, honey. He made sure we had copies of my latest sonogram and notes from my last visit with him to provide to local doctors in case I went into labor. And he recommended a beach trip to Lake Michigan instead of Florida."

Keep me quiet, Lord, Greg prayed. This guy qualifies as borderline abusive. How could Courtney have been involved with him?

"Well, all's well that ends well," Courtney said soothingly. "Have you had a chance to do much shopping, Leslie? I'd be glad to meet up tomorrow and give you a retail tour. Seems to me you could do with a babymoon gift. And then a push present. I know some excellent jewelers!"

Relieved and grateful for Courtney's seeming kindness, Leslie declined. "We leave in the morning, Court. It will be a long drive, but Drew's a peach about stopping when I need a potty break. Maybe we'll get down here again in a few months. I'd love to get together."

Greg shuddered at what the young woman was in for. Marriage to Drew was going to be hellish. Thank God Courtney had been betrayed. And thank God she'd gotten away from Drew. He'd have lured her back the instant he got bored with Leslie.

Making polite farewell noises, Greg and Courtney waved the couple off as they descended the dock stairs. Courtney turned to Greg and said, "Thanks for playing along, Greg. I had this sudden urge to do what I did. I'll ask God for forgiveness tonight, but for now I enjoyed myself no end."

"Let's get back to your place and 'process', as you psych types like to say," Greg said as he brushed his lips across her cheek. "I've just seen a side of you that shocked me senseless."

Stopping by his car, Courtney grabbed his face and kissed him so long that others in the lot began to laugh. Finally embarrassed, she said, "I am a woman of many facets, dear Greg. Better get used to it."

Chapter Fourteen

After a silent ride to her condo, Courtney got Greg a glass of bubbled water and settled across from him in the living room rocker. "I'm ready to process. Although I doubt there's much you can't figure out."

Reaching over to hug her while he placed her on the sofa next to him, Greg looked at her expectantly. "Go for it, woman. What you did back on the dock was worthy of the best gamester on the planet. Did you need revenge so badly that you had to talk to Drew and Leslie? Were you showing them how well you were doing away from Indiana? Or maybe you were just showing me off to them, though I didn't merit an introduction which was curious."

Courtney knew Greg was hurt, and perhaps a little angry at her manipulative display of fake friendliness to the last two people she would ever feel friendly toward. She tried to explain, if only to herself. "Greg, I'll admit revenge was part of it. Could you believe how uncomfortable Leslie looked? She had no business traveling so far at this stage of her pregnancy.

"But it wasn't only revenge. I needed to get the message across to Drew that I knew what he'd done. That he'd come down here primarily to see me. You were probably right when you said he viewed me as a commodity to keep in his back pocket, to keep in reserve in case things fell apart with Leslie." Courtney fumbled with her chain necklace and continued. "I'm a tiny bit ashamed, but I'm also glad I did it. He can't pretend to himself any longer that I'm wasting away in Destin without him. I apologize for not introducing you. I decided at that moment that he didn't have the right to know you. You're too good for him."

Greg looked skeptical. "Really? I'm too good for him? That doesn't ring true, Court."

Hating herself for what she was about to admit, Courtney shrugged. "Fine. I didn't introduce you because I wanted him to think I had lots of guys in my life. He could wonder who you were, and if there were more men I'm seeing. If you weren't important enough to introduce, there were likely loads of eligible men around. Petty, huh?"

At Greg's skeptical look, she was forced to admit the real reason for her game playing. "I guess there's more," she admitted. "If I had introduced you, Drew would have asked what you do for a living. That's his go-to conversation gambit, usually because he's sure he can one-up whoever he's talking to. So, you would have said you own and run the Destin Diabetes Care Clinic, correct?"

"Well, yeah, because that's what I do."

"Don't you see? It looks like I've been trolling for a man who matches up to Drew professionally! Drew would have loved that. He'd be sure I was still in love with him since I'd found a guy doing the same type of work. And that's why it's so important to me to have my own job, totally separate from what you do, Greg. I'll never be interconnected with my partner's work again."

Shrugging even harder than Courtney had when the conversation started, Greg stared at her for a full minute. "I guess I understand. Yes, it's very petty. But I can't decide if I'm very important to you or totally insignificant. Which is it?"

That question needed no words to answer. Courtney spent the better part of the evening convincing Greg that he was no Drew Clifton substitute.

After the momentous, or odd, depending on your outlook, meeting with Drew and Leslie, Courtney went back to work. Grateful to God again for her new job, with its patient variety and multiple locales, she adapted to a new normal. Three evenings each week she was busy until seven with the eating disorders IOP. The other days she worked a combination of initial intake duty at the hospital mental health center and then handled a small caseload of her own. Knowing herself better now, she admitted she was not cut out to treat only patients with a single diagnosis. The CDCES credential had qualified her to treat people with diabetes, gotten her out of Gordon, and helped her to meet Greg, but variety was the spice of her life.

As she worked, she continued to grieve Minnie. The older woman's counsel had been golden, but Courtney was happy her friend was with God and her husband at last. Frequent phone calls to Sherry in Indiana filled the gap and reminded Courtney she'd taken her sister for granted lately. In addition, she'd neglected her maid of honor duties terribly. Sherry would be married in a few months and needed a bridal shower, pronto.

Tapping in Sherry's number after work one evening, Courtney tried to make up for lost time. "So, Sis, what's on your agenda three Saturdays from now?"

"The usual, I guess. Vacuuming, dusting, polishing, all that domestic goddess stuff." Sherry seemed surprised by the question. "Is there something you need, Court?"

"No, there's something I need to do, and I apologize for slacking as your MOH. If I used my special organizational powers, could you attend a shower in your honor that day?"

"I can squeeze you in," Sherry said with obvious delight. "Though, I'll have to warn you I've had two other showers already. The guest list might be a little thin. It's a bit much to invite folks to multiple showers *and* a wedding."

Feeling even more guilty at ignoring her duties, Courtney was ready with a strategy. "I'd assumed that would be the case, since I've been sending gifts to those events. I'm sorry I couldn't make it, but I promise to do better. Here's my plan – since my friends only have my reports of our lives together, the shower I'm going to host will be for my friends, as a way to meet you for the first time. And I'll be able to see them, too. What do you think?"

Doubt crept into Sherry's voice. "I'm not sure. It seems pushy, don't you think? Sort of like grubbing for gifts."

"No, I checked it out already with Annie Upton. If

anyone would be the one to call me off, it would be her. She was actually thrilled to be able to see you. And to be honest, I framed it as more of a party than a shower. No games, no stiff small talk, just people who care for each other and are glad to get better acquainted while celebrating true love."

"Well, I'll be happy to have you here," Sherry said. "It does sound like fun. Some of the pre-wedding tasks are getting onerous." Taking a moment to think, Sherry transitioned to some sisterly banter. "You sound great, by the way. Either the new job is the ultimate career victory or you're serious about someone. Someone as in your former boss, I'll wager."

"You should buy a lottery ticket, Sherry. Your instincts are spot on. Greg is the best. He even tolerated my games when we ran into Drew and Leslie a few weeks ago. Can you believe they were *here* on their honeymoon?"

"That explains a lot! I ran into Leslie at the grocery, and she looked tanned but tired. She's really swollen. She made a lot of sweet chat about what a wonderful time they'd had in Destin, but I had no idea you saw them."

"First, I saw Drew, at his insistence. He pretended to want forgiveness. Then Greg and I saw both of them on a sunset cruise. As I said, Greg was a prince. I laid it on thick, like Leslie and I were besties. I was done with Drew but seeing what he put her through to come to Florida iced the cake for me. He's really awful."

"You have no idea," Sherry said. "I couldn't get away from her at the store. She went on and on about how she's still working full time despite her blood pressure being high. According to Leslie, Drew's rationale for her working is so she won't get bored. Then she slipped it in by mistake I'm sure, that she carries the health care benefits for Drew so the clinic will have better cash flow. If that marriage lasts, it will only be due to Leslie's willingness to do whatever he tells her to do."

"God help her," Courtney answered. "I'm sincere in that prayer. She's going to need a lot of divine intervention. Or maybe God will intervene by giving her a backbone."

"Like He did with you, Courtney. Thankfully."

The rest of the chat was devoted to shower planning. Afterward, due to the miracle of texts and instant messages, Courtney soon had acceptances from everyone on her friend list, in addition to Lauren's and Annie's moms, Kristen's mom and sister, who would be in town visiting, and Kristen's stepdaughter, Sophie. Even Elaine Stanfield and little Courtney were thrilled to attend. Combined with Shelly's other bridal attendants, the group looked like a good mix. The party promised to be a fun affair, though Courtney hoped the attention would be on future bride and not herself. Annie had been dropping lots of hints about the "hunky guy" Leslie had seen Courtney with on the sunset cruise. And when Annie was on a mission for information, there was no avoiding her questions.

True to form, Courtney's phone rang a few hours later. Annie's name popped up on the ID, so Courtney was warned. Annie was up to something.

"Hey, Mrs. Upton. What's going on in Indiana?"

"More of the same, as you well know. The more important question is, what's going on in Florida?"

"I'm enjoying my new job and missing my friend

Minnie. Not much else to report."

"Liar. I've got it from the miserable pregnant newlywed herself that you've got a major looker in your life. Leslie said he was the quiet type, though." Annie paused and continued. "I'm guessing it was the guy in the photo from New Orleans, right?"

Laughing out loud, Courtney had to be honest. "He was quiet due to my instructions. I was playing with Drew, plus I didn't want him to know Greg was the director of a medical clinic. Make sense?"

"Maybe a little," Annie said. "Were you afraid Drew would think you'd set out to replace him with a similar guy? That he would feel you were going after someone like him because your heart was so badly broken?" Annie followed her question with gagging sounds.

"Exactly. Annie, you're a devious thinker like Drew, but you've got kindness and ethics in your corner. Greg was hurt and a little surprised at my vindictive nature. He's probably also wondering if I still care for Drew at some level."

"If that's the case, I'll straighten you out in a few weeks," Annie said, obviously in the middle of a noisy task. "Greg would have to be real scum for you to still be carrying a torch for Drew."

"What are you doing? It sounds like you've got a noise machine on full volume."

"I'm vacuuming up some candy I dropped," Annie said. "My sweet tooth has been acting up of late." More noises, then the sound of a cord being wrapped followed. "Okay, I'm sitting quietly now. There's one other thing. Why don't both you and Greg come to the shower? He needs to meet Sherry, since she's your only family."

"And you need to meet *him*, right? Annie, if he would be able to come, I'd expect you to be on your best behavior. No grilling him, no setting him up to fail with impossible questions, no implications that I could do better. Because I doubt I can." Courtney's wistful tone spoke volumes. She realized Greg was the best man she'd ever known.

"What? I would be the epitome of decorum," Annie sputtered. "And besides, my mother will be at the shower, remember? She'll get the scoop on Greg for me. You know Rose."

Yes, I do, Courtney thought. Rose Dolce made Annie look tame. Maybe she'd discourage Greg from traveling to Indiana. Air fares were pricey, and he'd probably not want to be away from the clinic. She could only hope.

Greg called Eric on Saturday. His father had cancelled their usual golf outing, saying he was having lunch with a friend. Greg still needed to talk, so they made plans for Eric to come by after his lunch.

Serving his dad a cold drink after he declined anything to eat, Greg jumped in. "Dad, Courtney and I are pretty serious. Real serious. I love her and she loves me, which you already knew a while back. It took me longer to figure things out. I'm pretty sure Courtney's figured some things out as well." He told his father about Drew's visit, his seeking faux remorse and need for forgiveness, and the sunset cruise with his new wife. As Greg talked, Eric rubbed his face.

"Men like that give us all a bad name!" Eric shouted. Gathering himself, he said, "Even at my age, I'm appalled at how some women are treated by those who supposedly love them. Thank goodness Courtney is out of that man's clutches."

Since Eric rarely shouted and had never discussed sociopathic men with him in the past, Greg knew something was up. "What's her name, Dad? You might as well tell me. She's the 'friend' you had lunch with, right?"

Eric's face lit up. "Right. Her name is Jackie, and you see her five days a week. She left her husband after their younger son graduated from college in January. You didn't have a clue?"

No, he hadn't had a clue. Once again, his single-minded focus on work had caused him to ignore the pain of his most valued employee. Jackie had asked for a few days off a couple of months ago, citing "meetings downtown", but Greg hadn't even asked if there was anything she needed. No matter: clearly his dad had been able to help Jackie through the difficult time.

Recovering, he smiled at his father. "How serious is it, Dad? Ordinarily I'd advise caution since she's so recently divorced, but you've known each other for years. Any plans for an engagement? Marriage? Or am I jumping the gun?"

Greg smiled again and marveled at how happy he was for his father. This falling in love was powerful stuff. The two McClure men were in deep with their women. "Actually, I was going to bring up marriage, to Courtney of course, and ask about Mom's ring. But perhaps I'd better back off that plan."

"Yes, maybe you should. Jackie and I are in the early stages, but we know each other well, as you said. At my time of life, I'm inclined to marry sooner rather than later, but I think she's a little hesitant. Her ex was a real character. Treated her and the kids like they were invisible, while he burnished his stellar image in the community. She's always having to deal with intrusive questions about why she left him, as if no one in their right mind would let a man like him go."

Eric grimaced and continued, "As a matter of fact, another of her concerns has been your reaction. Does your smile indicate you're happy for us?"

"Very happy, Dad. May I tell Jackie that on Monday? I'll pretend we need to meet about insurance billings. No one in the office needs to know until the two of you decide to make your status public." He had a sudden dread of what Jessica would say when she heard the news. "And, Dad, we'd better remind Jackie about Jessica's probable reaction. She can be way over the top at times."

The men laughed, each wondering silently what Jessica would do if her former and current bosses both announced their intentions to marry. It would be festive to say the least.

"There's one more concern, Dad. Do you think Jackie will share Courtney's reservations about working for a family member?"

Eric smiled so broadly his face had to hurt. "No problem there, son. Jackie is happy to retire a little early, so you'll have a tough hiring task ahead. We've discussed traveling, taking gourmet cooking lessons, and even attending some major league baseball games. Can you believe she's a Cubs fan, like us?"

After a pause, Eric clapped his hands. "I've got it! Your mother not only had a beautiful engagement ring, which I'll have reset for Jackie when the time is right, but she also had a pretty diamond pendant necklace. You'd be welcome to that, if you'd want the stone for Courtney."

Touched by his father's happiness and generosity, Greg got up and hugged him. "Dad, that would be great. I appreciate it. And I have a feeling Mom is up there in heaven happy for us both."

Eric made his way to the door, and the two men shook hands. Greg shrugged and hugged his father again. "Dad, I'm as happy for you as I am for myself. You've covered your grief and loneliness well, but I've been worried about you when I could spare a second from worrying about my own challenges. I guess God takes care of us, despite our pain."

"You bet, Greg. Never forget that."

As Eric left, Greg's phone rang. Courtney's name was a welcome sight on the screen. "Dr. Bledsoe, we were just talking about you," he teased. "My only conclusion is that you were also eager to talk to me."

"Always, but I'm curious. Who is 'we' and what were you saying?"

"The topic is a secret, but I can tell you I was talking to my dad. I've got big news. He's in love, and you'll never guess with who."

"I'll bet it's Jackie," Courtney said. "She's been getting calls from Eric since her ugly divorce. I was praying they'd discover each other in a new way, separate from their history as employer-employee."

Marveling at Courtney's insight, Greg sighed. "You knew? I had no clue."

"Not a shock, my love. You've been preoccupied with the clinic, Taryn, and getting over my sudden departure. Not to mention realizing how good we are together, just not at the office."

"Then what's on your mind? Can we get together tonight?"

"I've got something for you to think about," Courtney hedged. "If you want to say no, there will be no hard feelings."

"I'm sure it's no big deal. Just ask."

"Well, I'm giving my sister a bridal shower in a few weeks. I'll be making a quick trip to Gordon for that, just a weekend thing. Sherry would like to meet you, and my protective friends would like to also."

Greg waited for Courtney to continue. He knew there was more.

"You'll need to be prepared. My friends and Sherry are very loyal. They hated what Drew pulled and want to screen you. They're the best people you'll ever meet, but very skeptical about my choice of men after Drew." Courtney groaned. "Although they were fooled by him, just as I was."

"I'm invited to Indiana to be interviewed for the job of Courtney's new man? I'm honored, actually. You should book flights when we hang up. And we should discuss the job description I'm interviewing for. Is it more than boyfriend, but less than fiancé?"

Courtney choked on the tea she had been sipping. "Well, you're way more than a casual boyfriend, Greg. You know that. I love you. Beyond that is your call."

"I'm ready to make that call," Greg said. "I'll be at your place at six." After ending the call with Courtney, he called his father and arranged to pick up the diamond pendant. It was time.

Chapter Fifteen

Courtney straightened her condo and trimmed chicken breasts for an easy dinner with Greg. She marinated them in an oil and balsamic herbal mix and readied rice pilaf and green salads. Dessert would be oatmeal-raisin cookies she'd baked a few days ago. She was too nervous to cook anything more complicated. What could Greg have meant when he said he was "ready to make that call"?

Greg arrived early, which was unusual for him. After a lengthy welcoming kiss, Courtney led them both to her balcony for appetizers. She'd gone the simple route again – mixed nuts and dried fruits from the pantry were all she could muster. If she'd tried to cut vegetables, she'd have risked injuring herself.

"Are you okay?" Greg asked. "You seem a little jumpy."

"I'm fine. Just a little edgy. Anything new other than your dad's big news?"

"No, just some things between us that need to be clarified."

Courtney's heart jumped. He was going to dump

her, she was sure. When she'd said she loved him on the phone, he hadn't responded in kind. She's served her purpose. His clinic was on firm financial footing, he'd found a good psychologist to replace her, and there was no reason to keep seeing her. Could she have misjudged this wonderful man? Not again!

Pulling herself together, she resolved to be calm. "What needs to be clarified?"

Greg took a pouch from his pocket. "This belonged to my mother. I want you to have it, Courtney. Not as is but reset into a ring. I love you, and I want to be with you always. Will you marry me?" He took the pendant from its container and put it in her hand.

Tears welled in Courtney's eyes. Then they spilled over, and she found herself wiping them away with the velveteen jewelry pouch. "Yes, I'll marry you! I love you so much, Greg. I was just afraid you were going to end things between us. You were so distant when we talked!"

Kissing her into silence, they enjoyed the moment for several minutes. Greg spoke first. "I'm sorry about that. When you mentioned meeting your sister and friends in Indiana, I realized Dad's happiness didn't have to be his alone. We belong together, Court. I knew the minute I saw you at the office on that horrendous first day. Then later at the hospital when you were wearing those tight jeans." His eyes gleamed and he winked. "But I was really sure when I saw you in the blue dress in New Orleans. You rock that dress, woman."

"You just love me for my appearance? What if I gain a lot of weight when I'm pregnant, like Leslie? Will I still be rocking my maternity jeans?"

Offended, Greg stood. "There's no way I would treat you like Drew is treating his wife. To have a woman carry my child is the best gift from God. Have I mentioned he's scum?"

"You have, a time or two," Courtney said between chuckles and tears. "Now let's see that diamond. I have some thoughts about a setting for a ring." She examined the stone, which appeared to be just under a carat in weight. "My mom had a pair of diamond earrings with smaller stones than this one. When our parents passed, Sherry got Mom's engagement ring and I received the earrings. We could make a three-stone ring from our moms' combined pieces that would be beautiful and carry lots of meaning to both of us."

Greg looked concerned. "Are you sure? I want you to have a big, gaudy ring when we go to Indiana." He paused, knowing he'd given himself away. "Not that I'm the competitive type, but what's Leslie's ring look like?"

"A three-stone ring with a combined weight of just under two carats will be plenty gaudy, mister," Courtney said as she took his hand in hers. "I have no idea what Leslie's ring is like. And it doesn't matter. My ideal man loves me, which is all that does matter."

Dinner was finished quickly, and Greg was anxious to give a local jeweler some business. They scrambled to his car and were at the store in a few minutes, each in possession of their mothers' diamonds. After a quick trip to the store and then explaining their needs to the man working the counter, the discussion began.

"I love the classic settings," Courtney said. "Just

three stones in a thin band, simple and elegant." She was sure the stones' beauty would be best highlighted with no distracting smaller gems.

The salesman, Damon, tried his best. "Wouldn't you like to see some halo settings? Or this one, with diamonds down each side of the shank?"

Greg jumped in. "I agree, Court. Those mountings sure add to the sparkle."

"No, I really like the graceful look of the plain band. It looks best on my somewhat short, stubby fingers." She kissed Greg on the cheek, and he seemed mollified.

Giving it one last effort, the salesman moved to the wedding band section of the counter. "Perhaps a jeweled wedding band would serve to add 'sparkle' to the plainer engagement ring. What do you think?" He showed them a tray of bands with diamonds across the top, all the way around, and with curled and braided effects.

Greg looked eagerly at Courtney. She hated to disappoint him, but she was going to. "Honey, I just want a plain thin gold band. I'm a baker, remember? I can't knead dough with the rings in this display. They'd be gunked up in no time and would be very difficult to clean."

"Understood," Greg said. "The simple set suits you well and not because your fingers are short. They're fine. But let's look at some earrings, since we have your Mom's pair to replace. They'll be your wedding gift, but you can wear them a little early when we go to Gordon."

Knowing when to count her victory and let Greg have his, Courtney hugged her fiancé. "Nice move, Greg. What a lovely idea. I'll look very impressive at Sherry's bridal shower. But let's look at simple settings for the earrings, okay? I love diamond stud earrings."

"Sure," Greg said as Damon moved to the earring and necklace section of the store. Moving close to Courtney as they followed, he whispered, "Studs to match the stud you're marrying, right?"

Laughing so loudly that Damon turned around, Courtney looked at her intended. "Oh, you're good. Very good."

The trip to Indianapolis required a change of planes in Atlanta. The quick stop allowed Greg to stretch his legs, buy Courtney a soft drink, and marvel at the many folks who traveled by air. They all seemed so matter of fact, as if flying at forty-thousand feet was a routine thing. Perhaps it was, but Greg was always amazed at the power of God's glory as the plane rose above the cloud cover and the beauty of the sky was revealed. It served as a good reminder of the insignificance of his problems and of the need to focus more on making life better for those in his world.

Later, as the jet descended to Indianapolis, Courtney studied him carefully. "Greg, are you okay? You're looking a little intense. Have no fear – meeting my friends and sister will be a breeze. They're the best, as are you. Your family is about to expand."

He hadn't been concerned about meeting the Hoosiers in Courtney's life. His thoughts were focused on Drew. Would they come into contact with each other? Or with Leslie? How would he react? What would he say to the man who betrayed the woman he now loved? Greg chuckled. He'd say *thanks*.

Stroking Courtney's temple, Greg smiled. "No such worries, Court. Just wondering what it will be like when we're in Indiana. Do you imagine we'll run into anyone else from your past life?"

Understanding his question beyond its seeming innocence, Courtney grinned back at him. "You never know. Gordon is a small town. If you're really asking about Drew, I'd say the odds are small. He's not one to go to the grocery or frequent the big box store on the weekend looking for power tools. When he's not at his clinic he stays around his house. As I say that, I realize what a narrow person he is. He has no interests outside of work and the financials that come with it. Of course, maybe now he's focused on Leslie." Courtney shook her head and added, "For her sake, I hope that's the case. I hate what she did, but she deserves a good husband."

Gratified that Courtney didn't care whose husband Drew was, Greg hugged her to him. "Thanks for that, sweetheart. Beyond the possible sighting of a certain physician, what can I expect? Tell me about Sherry."

After deplaning with their carry-on luggage and loading their rental car, Courtney obliged. "Sherry is my best friend. That says it all. Our personalities are a good complement to each other. As you know, I'm wound a little tight. She's loose and takes things as they come." Courtney frowned. "I've never understood that approach to life! My thinking is that you control every possible thing that you can, because unexpected things happen all the time."

"Like when your parents died?"

"Like that, yes, but also everything else that life

can throw at you. You never know what's coming next."

"I guess that's where faith comes in," Greg said, between glances at the car's speedometer. "As long as we do our part, God gets us through the pain. We have to remember that God is God."

"You sound like Jessica and Minnie," Courtney said.

"Who? Jessica, who runs my office ragged with her emotional outbursts? When she heard about my dad's engagement, Jackie threatened to leave for the day if Jessica didn't calm down."

"Despite her enthusiastic nature, Jessica is a deep thinker. And a good person."

"Whatever you say," Greg agreed. "Where should I head when we get to Gordon? Sherry's or the hotel?"

"Let's go to Sherry's. She's going to have dinner ready for us, and you'll meet her fiancé, Patrick."

As they pulled into the drive of Sherry's (and soon to be Patrick's) home, the couple greeted them outside the door. Hugs and introductions were exchanged, and over drinks the foursome became better acquainted. That is, the men heard a lot about the Bledsoes and their formative years. They also learned about the deceased Bledsoe parents, universally described as almost saintly, salt-of-the-earth types. Greg picked up on the things left unsaid.

"What are you leaving out?" he asked. "Even my mom did some unforgettable things when I tested her too many times. Once she spanked me so hard my dad had to intervene. Of course, against her direct orders I'd climbed a tree, gotten an egg out of a robin's nest, and then broke it all over my new suede cowboy jacket."

Once the laughter ended, Courtney admitted a few of her parents' flaws. "They loved to party with their friends. The eighties were a fun-loving time. The morning after one particularly festive night, Mom and Dad had a huge fight about him driving home after having too many drinks. The party hostess had over-served him all night, and Mom was convinced she was flirting with him. He was still such a traditionalist that he wouldn't let Mom take the wheel. She was livid." Courtney's earlier grin was replaced with a flash of sadness. "I thought they were going to get a divorce. I asked Mom about it, and her reply was that she'd never let him off that easy! She hugged me and told me not to worry, but to marry a man who knew his limits."

Sherry eyed Greg and asked, "So, Dr. McClure, what is your stance on alcohol consumption?"

"My stance is that it's fine for others but does me no good," he replied. "I had some awful benders in college." After locking eyes with Courtney, he winked. "I know my limits."

After a dinner of grilled trout and spinach salad, Courtney and Greg said their goodbyes and headed for the hotel. "We've got an early morning tomorrow," Courtney said. "I've got lots to do. In addition to setting up for the shower, I need to soothe Sherry. She hates being the center of attention, which is the whole point of the party. Thank goodness Rose Dolce agreed to host at her place. She has more room than Sherry and is even making Italian pastries for dessert. I've had the meal catered, though it nearly killed me to do so. I would have loved to cook for everyone." Squelching a sigh, she added, "And you, my friend, have a golf date with all of your new Indiana best friends, meaning the husbands of my buddies. Bryan, Mike, and Ben are great guys. Patrick will help you negotiate all the new personalities. And Mike is a doctor like you, so you'll have that in common."

Thinking that golf sounded way better than Courtney's morning, Greg kissed her goodbye. People were people, he thought. Indiana or Florida. Courtney's people were good folks. Of course, they were. They all loved her, and she loved them.

Courtney's concerns were silly. Rose had the shower details under control, and the luncheon was fabulous. The highlight, of course, was dessert. Rose's pastries were phenomenal, and the guests' low-carb diets went out the window for the afternoon. After everyone had eaten their fill, Courtney got the party rolling.

"Okay, everyone, I know we all detest shower games. But what's a shower without tedious rivalry? We will play one word game, an oldie but goodie." Courtney passed out papers and pens to all the guests, amid groans and eye rolls. "At the top of the page is the phrase 'Bridal Party'. The challenge is to make as many words as you can within from that phrase in five minutes. And you already have two words on your list – 'Bridal' and 'Party'. Time begins now!"

Muttering ensued, but the attendees gave in to their competitive natures. Rose Dolce was declared the winner with over twenty words. Scoffing at the amazed guests, she said, "I read a lot, ladies. There's no better way to enhance your vocabulary than to read. Take note, Sophie and Courtney S."

The two little girls smiled at the mention of their names, but Sophie took Courtney B aside as Sherry moved to begin opening her gifts. "Courtney B, I guess I understand why you had to have a game. But it was too much like school. Next time, have a fun game, okay? My mommy Kristen told me about a toilet paper game she played once at a shower. That would be way better." Little Courtney S nodded in serious agreement, clearly yielding to the older and more sophisticated Sophie Sutliff.

"Good suggestion, Sophie. I'll remember that for the next shower I host." She hugged both girls. "And thanks to you both for coming. Sometimes grown-up parties aren't much fun, but you were troopers. I'll cut you the corner pieces of cake, the ones with the most frosting."

At that moment, the golf group entered Rose's living room. "We wanted to see what kind of loot my bride is getting," Patrick said. "And of course, there's cake to be had."

The men made themselves comfortable, with Greg sitting close to Courtney as he took her hand. Rose eyed the pair and made it her business to switch seats with Kristen, who had been on Courtney's other side.

"We seem to be under the microscope," he whispered. "Should I be concerned about Mrs. Dolce?"

"I'm not sure," Courtney said. "She's been sort of a surrogate mom to Sherry and me since our parents died. But she's a good-hearted soul. She just wants us to be happy. Patrick had to pass muster with her, so I suppose you do as well."

"Great," Greg muttered.

After the loot Patrick mentioned had been un-wrapped and admired, the party began to break up. Soon the only guests remaining were Courtney and Greg.

"Greg, why don't you go back to the hotel?" Rose asked, though it was more an order than a question. "Courtney and I will do some catching up, and I'll bring her back to you. You probably need a shower after a hot morning on the golf course."

Knowing he'd been dismissed and wondering if he had an offensive smell, Greg obeyed and headed out the door. "See you later, Court," he said with a wave.

Puzzled, Courtney looked at Rose. "What's up, Rose? I thought the party was lovely, and it was fun to have all my friends and their husbands together. Thanks again for letting us use your home."

"Nothing's up," Rose said. "I just wanted to chat for a while. We haven't talked in so long."

When each woman had a fresh mug of coffee, Rose continued. "I was anxious to meet Greg. I ex-pected a boyfriend, but he's your fiancé!"

Feeling guilty at Rose's scrutiny and not knowing why, Courtney sipped her drink. "It happened just a few weeks ago, Rose. Our feelings had been build-ing, but we had a rocky start. Greg was just ending a relationship. As you know, it took me a while to get Drew out of my system."

"Probably so," Rose said, brows arched. "Tell me about Greg."

"He's wonderful," Courtney gushed. "He's made the clinic a success while negotiating a very difficult health care environment. He treats his employees with respect and pays them above standard wage.

His dad, Eric, is a sweetheart. They've become closer since Greg's mom died."

"It's interesting, though, that Greg and Drew have so much in common. Both doctors, both running their own clinics, each ambitious and successful."

Courtney stared at the older woman. "They don't have much in common at all, Rose. I suppose their professions are similar, but Greg is nothing like Drew. Surely you know that."

"No, I don't. Their professions are remarkably similar. They both seem to be full of confidence. You were linked to Drew professionally and to Greg for a while, too. *Lots* of things in common."

"Again, Rose, they're nothing alike." As she shifted on her chair, Courtney's irritation showed as she spilled a bit of coffee on the side table. "I can understand why you'd think so at first glance but let me repeat, Greg is nothing like Drew. He's honorable and fair. He and his father support each other. And he understood why I wanted to have a career separate from his, not just due to my history with Drew, but because I needed a job with variety and growth potential."

Rose nodded as she wiped up Courtney's spill. "Good to hear, Courtney." She stood and gently kissed Courtney's cheek. "I suppose I had to interrogate you a little, since your mom's gone."

"Okay. I guess I understand. But Greg's the best, Rose. There's no one better for me."

"Maybe you do understand, partly. But I needed to be sure you loved Greg beyond all reason, you know? And can you see why?"

"Not really. I get that you're looking out for me, after Drew's betrayal."

"I *am* looking out for you, but not for the reason you think. I'm also looking out for Greg. He's a wonderful man. It's obvious he's crazy about you." Rose leaned toward Courtney and took her hands. "I wanted to be sure you were committed to Greg, because Drew will be seeking you out again. I give his marriage a year at best. He'll betray that silly nurse and leave his baby without a thought, while blaming it all on his wife."

Noting Courtney's attempt to pull her hands away, Rose held her grip and went on. "Drew is nothing like Greg, as you already know. I had hopes for Drew and his father. I believed they had changed, that they were men of honor. But I know that's not true. In fact, Dan Clifton is being sued for divorce by his wife, Vanessa. She couldn't take his ego and cheating anymore. It's sad, but Drew is becoming just like his dad."

Squeezing Rose's hands, Courtney released them and stood. "The Cliftons are divorcing? That's so sad, for them and for Drew. But it's got nothing to do with me." She studied the family portrait on Rose's mantle. "To the world, they look like your family in this picture. Loving, perfect, successful. But I don't agree with your other point. Drew will never seek me out."

Rose grunted loudly and punctuated the sound by raising her arms to heaven in frustration. "Just wait, missy. In fact, he's already done it. Annie told me about his 'honeymoon' in Destin. Florida's a big state with endless miles of beachfront, but he chose to be in your city."

"I know that, Rose. That visit wasn't about getting back together with me, though. I think Drew had to see me, in hopes that I was a grieving mess. He wanted me to be a lost, hopeless woman. That's hardly the same as getting back together."

"Trust me, it will happen. I wanted to be sure of your commitment to Greg. I feel better now." Satisfied that she'd done her job, Rose smiled sweetly at Courtney.

Courtney laughed. "Wait a minute! You were protecting Greg, not me? You never cease to amaze, Rose. Thanks for your loving interference!"

"It's my specialty, Courtney. Just ask my daughter."

Chapter Sixteen

Sunday morning dawned bright and clear. "Good weather to fly home," Greg said as they ate their breakfast. "How are we going to spend the morning?"

Courtney's phone jingled. She read the text and replied. "Looks like our morning has been planned for us. You've got a date at the putting green with the guys. I'm headed to Sherry's for a mysterious meeting with the girls. We can rendezvous there at one and head to Indy for our four o'clock flight."

After Greg changed into putting gear, Courtney kissed him goodbye. "I sure hope you're not walking into another confrontation with Rose," Greg said. "I've passed her test, but she may have changed her mind."

"No matter," Courtney said with another, more passionate kiss. "You're my man, whether you like it or not."

"I like it. I like it a lot." They got in the rental car and sped away to Sherry's.

Greg dropped Courtney off and waved to the women gathered on the porch. Courtney felt ambushed and asked, "What's up, ladies? Surely you're not going to challenge my engagement to the best guy in the world."

"You're so paranoid, but in all fairness, my mom tends to have that effect on people," Annie said. "This is a fun confab. It's a tradition among us – we discuss your wedding gown and help you figure it out."

"I *figured* I'd head to a store in Destin and buy something suitable for the beach," Courtney said. "You're all invited, of course, but it's going to be a small, informal affair. Destin has lots of options for dresses."

"But so do we," Kristen said. "In fact, we want you to try on the dress Annie wore to her wedding." Kristen explained she had purchased the Grecian gown from a prom display when she didn't think she would be able to find a dress for her wedding to Mike. Instead, Lauren had stepped in and altered her original dress to fit Kristen. Annie wore the ivory pleated "toga" gown to her wedding with Ben. "Now it's time to repurpose Annie's gown for you. It would be a perfect beach dress. And we're not being pushy. If you don't like the dress, that's okay. But why not give it a try? Even though you're living in Destin, you're one of the Gordon tribe."

Courtney gulped back tears. "Thank you all so much. Sherry, are you okay with this? Maybe the toga dress would be better for you."

"I'm fine, Court. I'm wearing Patrick's sister's dress. It's gorgeous. It cost thousands of dollars and I didn't spend a penny. It didn't even need alterations! Annie's dress has your name on it."

Courtney went to Sherry's bedroom and tried on the gown on loan from her former buddy at GCC.

It fit well, with a shorter train effect since she was slightly taller than Annie. She paraded out to the living room to get the group's feedback.

Lauren, once again serving as part-time dress designer, looked at Courtney with a critical eye. "It fits perfectly in the bodice, and for the beach the shorter train is perfect. No sense in dragging more sand around than you have to." She stood by Courtney and focused on the one-shoulder design. "I'm not sure if this is the best look for you, however. I can take this piece off and bring the dress back to the original bodice – a sweetheart neckline to enhance your 'attributes'. God has gifted you with a fine figure."

The group laughed, with Annie the first to comment, "Yes, Greg will like the revealing neckline better. I went with the one-shoulder design because I was afraid of my mom's reaction to a sexy dress. And Ben didn't care what I wore, as long as we got married asap."

Lauren produced a pair of scissors and within minutes Courtney saw the full effect of the new neckline. "It's gorgeous! I'm beyond grateful." She walked to the bedroom mirror to get the full effect. "Yes, it's perfect as is. Thanks, Lauren."

"We're not finished yet," Lauren said. "Annie's heavy jeweled belt is too fancy for a beach wedding. I'm thinking floral ribbon, or maybe an embroidered lace peplum with sequins to sparkle in the sun. Give me a few days, and I'll text you some photos."

Courtney's tears couldn't be held back. "What did I do to deserve such good friends?" she asked. "You've almost got me ready to move back here." She wiped her eyes, adding, "But not really. Florida has

Greg, warm winters, and the ocean."

"If you like that sort of thing," Annie groused. "On the other hand, I just love the scenic corn fields, bundling up like an Eskimo from November to March, and arguing with macho Hoosier men." She paused and added, "Well, there's one macho guy I do like to argue with, because then we get to make up."

Footsteps ended the discussion about the merits of Indiana vs. Florida. Courtney hustled to the bedroom to change before Greg entered the room. Lauren followed.

"Court, we haven't talked about your veil," she said. "Have you given that any thought?"

"It's usually too windy on the beach for a veil. Maybe a floral headpiece? Or a headband? I'm not into bridal fashion like you are."

"Leave it to me," Lauren said. "When I mail you photos of the dress, I'll include options for your headwear. Or you could opt out of them altogether." She paused and gently placed her hands on Courtney's shoulders. "You get to choose, Court. Just like you chose Greg. Your mom's not here to give advice but based on what I've seen, you chose very well."

They hugged and left the bedroom in time to see Greg tapping his foot and looking pointedly at his watch. "We've got to go, honey. Our flight will not wait for us, despite the importance of wedding planning."

The drive to the airport was smooth, with a minimal number of trucks trying to pass while simultaneously camping in the left lane. Once secure in their airplane seats, Greg turned to Courtney.

"I've got a huge favor to ask, and since we're on a public flight and it's frowned on to yell at your fiancé, I'm going to broach this topic now."

What could be the problem? Courtney was sure the trip had gone smoothly. Everyone had loved Greg, especially Rose. Why would Greg think she'd yell at him? "Go ahead. I can take it. Talk to me, Greg."

"It's a good problem to have, I guess. It means my dad loves us beyond reason. And Jackie's okay with it."

Still puzzled, but sensing she might know what was coming, Courtney smiled. "And?"

"I called Dad yesterday after my golf date, before the guys went to your shower. He was thrilled about our plans for a beach wedding and when I texted him today, he was touched at your friends giving you a gown. Then, out of the blue, he suggested a double wedding for the four of us. I think it's his way of cementing us all as a family. And maybe he's a little threatened about your Indiana ties. He doesn't want us to move away." Greg sucked in a deep breath and gripped the hand rests.

After a moment, Courtney smiled at Greg. "Well, Jane Austin would approve." Laughing at Greg's puzzled look, she said, "In *Pride and Prejudice*. The two sisters had a double wedding."

Courtney looked out the windows at the clouds swirling around the jet. "In many ways, Jackie was my substitute mom when I started at the clinic. She was kind to me when I interviewed and ran a lot of interference when you and I were battling. She could also tell I was full of angst about an old relationship. We had several good talks during lunch hours. And your dad is wonderful. I'd love to have a wedding with them, provided you do too."

"I'd share a wedding with an Elvis impersonator,"

Greg muttered. "I just want to get married. You Indiana women make things extra challenging."

After kissing him across the empty middle seat, Courtney said, "We're worth it."

Greg looked at his scheduled appointments. The long weekend in Indiana had been good for both him and Courtney. She'd blossomed at seeing her friends, he'd enjoyed their banter and obvious love for each other, and Rose had deemed him acceptable for her substitute daughter. In a few short weeks (or months), he and Courtney would be husband and wife. His dad would also be a married man again. Jackie's presence in his father's life was a true miracle; after assuming his dad would be a single man forever, Greg realized Eric had plenty of life and love left to give. Which was how it should be. Life was meant to be lived with love and purpose.

Jackie, (soon to be his stepmother!) poked her head into his office. "Greg, Cathy Eller is on line one. She sounds a little distraught."

Great. It would be like Mandy to go into a crisis just as his life was in a good place. For some reason, that kid had gotten under his skin more than any other patient in his career. Perhaps it was because he and Courtney had connected for the first time when they saw Mandy in the hospital. He hoped the teen was all right.

"Dr. McClure here," he said. "Cathy, what's up?"

"Thanks for taking my call," she said. "My cell is out of juice, and I don't have a charger with me. I'm using the staff phone."

"Are you at the hospital?"

"Yes, we've been here all night," Cathy said. "Mandy had a terrible day yesterday. She complained of her stomach hurting and then she began to vomit." She choked back a sob and continued. "I'm ashamed to say I thought she was faking illness to get out of a test at school."

"Was she making herself throw up?" Greg hoped not, but he had to ask. Courtney would be discouraged if Mandy had taken yet another step backwards.

"No, not at all, but I understand your question. Turns out she had a burst appendix, Dr. McClure. Dr. Sanderson said she'll be fine, but I wanted your opinion."

"Rachael Sanderson is a great surgeon," Greg said. "She'll take good care of Mandy." Recalling Cathy's own trauma in losing her husband and caring for Mandy, he asked, "How are you doing, Cathy?"

"I'm holding up," she answered. "Not my best two days, but not the worst. I'll be looking forward to telling my counselor all about this. When I was afraid of losing Mandy, I did my deep breathing and called my prayer chain partner at church. It helped a lot. My counselor will be proud."

As he was ending the call, Jackie's face again appeared in his doorway. "Now you've got a call on line two," she said, smiling. "This one will be more pleasant."

"Dr. McClure," he said into the phone.

"Is that any way to greet your beloved wife-to-be?" Courtney teased. "I wanted to fill you in on the latest about Mandy Eller. She's in the hospital, but not due to a relapse."

"I just talked to Cathy. Sounds like Mandy will be fine. But thanks for calling me. How is your day going?"

"My day is infinitely better now that I've spoken to you. I'll be a little late for our dinner, though. I'm going to stop by the hospital to see Mandy and Cathy. Even though Mandy finished the IOP, I figure they both need some support."

"Good idea. Why don't we both go, then head out to dinner?"

They made plans to meet at the hospital at six and then find a nearby restaurant after the visit. Greg's chest warmed at the thought of marrying Courtney soon. Unlike other brides he'd heard about, the wedding planning was seamless. She had her dress, recently received from Lauren, and she and Jackie had made a perfect team. The sunset ceremony was all set, complete with dinner and dancing to follow at a hotel restaurant close by.

Greeting Greg with a kiss in the hospital lobby, Courtney marveled at how much she loved her fiancé. God had taken care of her, despite her hopelessness and lack of faith when she'd moved to Destin. Thanking Him yet again, she knew Drew had been in her life for a purpose, if only to show her what a good man was like in comparison to him. She wasn't sure if things happened for a reason, but she was grateful Drew had led her to Greg.

"What's on your mind?" Greg asked. "You seem like you're trying to figure something out." They made a left turn and entered the surgery wing of the small hospital.

"Just saying a prayer of thanksgiving," she answered. "Here's Mandy's room."

As they entered, Mandy's voice greeted them. "I was hoping you'd come," she said. "And you came together! That's a good sign, right?"

Cathy tried to hush her daughter, but Courtney laughed and put her hands up. "Yes, we can give you some of the credit, Mandy. You were very effective when you made a point to tell each of us how miserable the other one looked." Pointing her engagement ring, she added, "You've got a manipulative streak, Ms. Eller. But we appreciate it all the same!"

Slipping into doctor mode, Greg spoke in low tones to Cathy. Apparently pleased at her responses, he focused on Mandy. "Everyone is swearing this wasn't an eating disorders relapse, young lady. Is that true?"

"Swear to God," Mandy said, eyes wide while she held her hand up and grasped an imaginary Bible. "I was following my meal plan, exercising moderately, and working the hostess desk at the restaurant." She shuddered and went on. "Waiting tables was too much temptation for me. You have to know your own limits," she concluded with a serious head nod.

"Sage advice," Courtney responded. "I'm so glad you're going to be okay. Keep in touch. Who knows? We might even ask you back to IOP to be a speaker on the advantages of staying healthy after major surgery."

"See what a good match you two are?" Mandy asked. "You cured me and found each other at the same time. Of course, I helped a lot!"

Epilogue

After Jackie adjusted Courtney's floral headband, Courtney returned the favor and pinned in Jackie's jeweled headpiece. Hugging her soon-to-be step-mother-in-law, Courtney laughed at the absurdity of the label. "I can't be calling you my 'stepmother-in-law', Jackie. How about just 'Mom'?"

Jackie's eyes filled. "That's wonderful, Courtney. You're like a daughter to me. We sure had an interesting beginning, didn't we?"

"Did we ever! Greg was on the warpath and you teased him just enough to deflect his anger about my being hired by his dad. Who would have predicted we'd be getting married now? Or that you and Eric would also? Life is so unpredictable."

"Truer words never spoken," Jackie said. "My journey has certainly had its share of hills and valleys. After my divorce, I thought I'd be content to work my job and putter around the house during my free time. God has given me so much, things I never would have even dreamed of at this stage of my life."

Courtney peeked out of the dressing room attached to the restaurant venue. She was touched by the turnout. All of the Diabetes Care Clinic staff members were there, as were other friends from Destin. Most touching for her was the large Indiana contingent. Everyone at the bridal shower for Sherry had made it, even Kristen's mom and sister from Arizona. Rounding out the list of folks from Indiana were Minnie's two daughters. Courtney realized she and Sherry had a family, even though they were "orphans". God was good, yet again. Of course, Jackie's family had also come. To a person, they were beaming their approval at Eric.

The musical interlude began with the string quartet performing songs chosen by the McClure men. Courtney and Jackie were touched by the music selections since each piece held special meaning for the two women and their men.

As if she knew she had been in Courtney's thoughts, Kaye Anderson leaned over to Katie and whispered, "This bit of nostalgia brings back a lot of memories." A lone tear escaped, despite her efforts to remain composed. "And seeing all of our friends from Gordon makes me so happy. I miss it all, honey. The seasons, the familiar places, and most of all, the people. Let's talk after the wedding, okay? I've been thinking Phoenix is more a place to snowbird than to live permanently."

Katie nodded and squeezed her mother's hand. "Yes, we'll talk more later."

When the music ended, Jackie kissed Courtney on the forehead and said, "Let's go get married, girl. We have two fine men waiting for us, with the perfect

Destin sunset as the backdrop." Her eyes glistened, and she was careful not to smudge her eye makeup.

Courtney blinked and did her own version of mascara smear prevention, holding her fingers under her eyes while she took a deep breath. "Enough of this, Jackie. There are two lucky men waiting on the beach for us."

At the appropriate time, signaled by Jessica's frantic wave, they stepped out of the room and walked hand in hand down the aisle, which was actually a sand path raked smooth and heavily scattered with flower petals.

The brides were a study in contrast. Courtney's strapless Grecian gown was both classic and sexy, having been altered to perfection by Lauren. She had added dual high side slits so each of Courtney's steps revealed a bit of tanned leg. Jackie's creamy silk sundress was topped with a seafoam green shawl with peacock motifs, matching the shades of the ocean water perfectly. To highlight their solidarity, identical pedicures in the same seafoam green color topped their bare toes. Eric smiled broadly at Jackie, while Greg looked at Courtney with a combination of wonder and desire.

"Yes, let's do this," Courtney said quietly. "We can't keep those two waiting any longer."

Discussion Questions

1. How would you characterize Courtney's move to Florida? Running away from the past? Moving toward the future? An exercise in self-care? A combination of these?

2. Greg didn't want to hire a psychologist, much less one as attractive as Courtney. Why did he overstep when he took her hand after the hospital visit with Mandy? Was Courtney's reaction appropriate?

3. The meeting in New Orleans heightened the chemistry between Courtney and Greg. Have you ever had an intense attraction to a person you didn't know well? How did things work out? Can a strong pull toward a virtually unknown person be the basis for a healthy relationship?

4. Jessica's "theology" helped Courtney think differently about her life. Have you ever had a friend or loved one offer an unusual perspective on your difficulties?

5. Courtney got acquainted with her neighbor, Minnie, who became another friend and

counselor. What did Minnie's life experiences have to offer Courtney? How did she challenge Courtney?

6. In addition to trust, Courtney had issues with grief. Her parents' deaths happened over five years ago, but she continued to suffer their loss. Does grief "resurface" in your life? As in Courtney's case, do recent losses magnify those long past? What helps you deal with feelings of sadness and betrayal?

7. Minnie's daughters hinted at her being a tough, even difficult, mother. Courtney's time with Minnie was more positive. Can both realities be valid? How have your own behaviors changed as you learn and grow?

8. Mandy's eating disorder was complicated by her diabetes. Her mother's unresolved feelings about Mandy's father also impacted Mandy's health. How has your own physical health been affected by your mood or stress level?

9. Rose Dolce was a powerful force during Courtney and Greg's visit to Indiana. In addition to vetting Greg, she confronted Courtney about her feelings toward Drew. Do you agree that Drew will try to return to Courtney?

10. Even after five years, Courtney missed her parents terribly, especially her mother. God helped, however. Jackie, Minnie, and Rose all served as substitute moms during Courtney's developing relationship with Greg. Has God ever provided for you in this way?

Dear Friends,

Thank you for reading *From Destin with Love*. I hope you enjoyed Courtney's journey from Indiana to Florida, along with getting to know the folks she met in Destin. I believe Courtney's path is common to all of us. Life doesn't turn out the way we'd hoped or planned, and it's tough to imagine God's hand in things when we're suffering. He persists, though, time and time again!

Take good care,
Leanne

A Look At:
Back Home For Love

When Katie and her mom, Kaye, move to Phoenix, AZ they thought it life would be great. No more harsh winters in Indiana. Too bad they forgot about loneliness and extreme heat.

Be careful what you wish for.

After attending the wedding in Destin and seeing so many old friends and family, both mother and daughter decide to move home.

When Katie gets a new job, she also meets a very stubborn man. The French Cuisine professor is more than she can handle. And he's not too hot for her, either. But when they work together on a project, both get more than they bargained for.

Kaye's even finding that moving home isn't as easy as she thought it would be. In order to keep busy, she joins the Healthy Living Club where an old foe is now the director. When these two cross paths, can Kaye learn to forgive?

Will either mother or daughter be able to forgive and move on? Or will their past experiences ruin their chances at happiness?

Come back to Gordon, Indiana one last time and see if spring flowers will bloom, or the harsh winter will keep hearts frozen.

About the Author

After a satisfying career as a psychologist, Leanne focused her efforts on writing novels that reflect her firm belief in God's love, grace, and provision. She and her husband live in Indiana and visit their daughter in South Carolina as often as possible. A homebody at heart, her life is full as long as there are family and friends in frequent contact, opportunities to travel, and books to be written.

The fourth novel in the Indiana Romance Series will be coming soon! Courtney has been a loyal friend to Annie during her romance with Ben, a devoted partner to Drew as he grows his psychiatry practice, and an ethical psychologist in her role as director of Counseling Services at Gordon Community College. Questions remain, however - the most important one being whether Drew is worthy of Courtney's love.

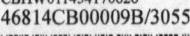